"A guy knows a princess when he's lucky enough to meet one."

Michael's voice was husky as he opened the door to his room. "Come to bed with me."

Katherine gasped. In the center of the room, an enormous, round bed hung on chains from the ceiling beams. It was covered with furs. "A round bed?"

"I kept bashing myself on the corners, so I rounded it." Like a knight who had just won his woman, Michael swooped her up into his arms. "You're the first woman who's ever been up here." The bed swayed on its hinges, rocking them.

"God, you feel good." He pulled her closer, running his hands down her back, then up under her sweater, pulling it over her head.

His skin was hot and intoxicating. The night wind howled, and she could hear the distant clicking . . . *of talons?* "Do you hear something?"

"The wind," he said.

Katherine shivered, but not from the cold. "I have this strong feeling that we're not alone."

Michael's voice sounded resigned. "The dragon."

Dear Reader,

Regan Forest creates the most intriguing, unusual and romantic stories as fans of her Harlequin Dreamscape novel *Moonspell* will attest! *The Lady and the Dragon* is a very special Temptation romance, bringing to vivid life our fantasies about knights in shining armor and damsels in distress—although our modern damsel does pretty well by herself! This magical story is justifiably an Editor's Choice.

The winged dragon is the symbol of Wales, and virtually every castle is considered haunted, although Regan hasn't heard of one being haunted by a dragon. Her background in anthropology was useful in plotting this story, since she had studied fossil hoaxes. So which is it, hoax or dragon? Read and find out—you won't be disappointed!

We would love to hear from you about *The Lady and the Dragon* and our other innovative Editor's Choice titles. Please take the time to write to us:

The Editors
Harlequin Temptation
225 Duncan Mill Road
Don Mills, Ontario, Canada
M3B 3K9

The Lady and the Dragon
REGAN FOREST

Harlequin Books

TORONTO • NEW YORK • LONDON
AMSTERDAM • PARIS • SYDNEY • HAMBURG
STOCKHOLM • ATHENS • TOKYO • MILAN

For Linda and Phillip Bennett
with thanks for their wonderful Welsh hospitality and
for the memories of tramping through haunted castles—
and finding the cave of the dragon!

Published July 1991

ISBN 0-373-25455-5

THE LADY AND THE DRAGON

1

"YOU'VE GOT TO STOP that woman from coming here. It's too dangerous," Michael said to the man behind him in a dank upper chamber of the castle tower. He pulled tape across the thick bandage on his upper arm and winced with pain.

His father poured himself another glass of whiskey. "Danger? From a thousand-year-old dragon? Do you take me for a doddering old fool? I know you want to weasel out of meeting Katherine, but I didn't think you'd invent a story to scare her off."

The weak electric lights dimmed, brightened and dimmed again. Michael poured himself a whiskey. *The damn generator is going again,* he thought. "I didn't want to tell you about the attack because of your heart condition. I figured Katherine's imminent visit was putting too much strain on you already."

"Bosh and slop. I'm sure you scraped your arm on a toolbox or fell down a flight of stairs."

"I wish I *could* explain what slashed my arm." The younger man settled onto an overstuffed sofa, propped his feet on the old chest in front of him and took a long drink. "There's something prowling around this castle at night and until we know who or what it is, we've got no business inviting a woman here. Especially someone like her. She sounds like the kind of woman who screams at the sight of a spider—much less a sharp-clawed dragon."

Michael Thomas, Sr., stroked his white beard. "The dragon is the reason Katherine and I met...and the reason she's coming. She's an expert on dragons, damn it."

"On myths, Dad. Our resident is no myth." Mike carefully rolled down the sleeve of his heavy wool shirt and bent his arm several times against the pain. His intense blue eyes met the equally intense eyes of his father. "You shouldn't have enticed her with those stories."

"She knew of the stories long before I started writing to her. Well, I'll admit, I told her what has taken place in the castle since I came—"

"If that isn't enticing, I don't know what is. I don't want a little old lady tottering around here. Our deal is off."

His father glared. "It's too late to back out. She'll be here in a week."

"Impersonation is against my principles. I was blitzed on whiskey when you talked me into your stupid charade. You took advantage of me, working on my sympathy."

The uncertain electric current dimmed the light that shone against two ancient tapestries hung on walls of stone. Depictions of the hunt, in frayed and faded dark-toned colors. Running horses, a terrified stag, men in wool and leather, English sporting spaniels—ancestors, perhaps, of the two English springers who occupied the castle today.

Within this tower—the medieval gatehouse tower—light glowed and a fire blazed, but the remainder of the ancient fortress remained empty, cold, uninhabitable. It slept in deep, shivering shadows of its bloody history, harboring among its many ghosts the much-feared ghost of a dragon.

In the arched, stone doorway that opened from the dark tower stairs the two springer spaniels paused to shake off sprays of rain from their thick coats before they sauntered into the room. The black-and-white dog, Talbot, plopped down on the rug by the fire, while the lighter, liver-and-white spaniel, Pembroke, went to Michael and laid her head against his thigh. He reached down to pet her wet head and soggy ears. "It's still raining," Mike said.

"Don't change the subject. This...charade as you call it may be the last favor I ever ask of you before I die." Thomas thudded his fist over his own heart. "Katherine thinks I'm much younger. I can't bear the humiliation of her finding an old man."

"You deliberately misled her."

"I never thought she'd actually come here! Look, I know I shouldn't have misled her, but it's too late to undo it now. Pretending to be me for a few days is little enough to ask. If she does need protection in the castle, you can guard her far better than I."

Mike scowled and pushed at the dog who had taken a lick from his whiskey glass. "And how do you plan to explain why the villagers call me Michael instead of Thomas?"

"No problem there. My correspondence with Katherine started out as rather official, so luckily I signed all my letters by my first name."

"Official? I have no doubt that this poor spinster thinks she's in love with you . . . which means me! And *I'm* not what she's looking for."

His father, sensing victory, smiled. "From the gossip, my boy, you are what every woman is looking for."

Mike winced. "And where'd you hear that?"

"In the village. The local girls have their eye on you, and don't pretend you're not aware of it. The handsome young American millionaire who's a castle lord."

"You mean one of the crazy Americans who bought a legend and can't pay the taxes on it or get what little is left of the roof to stop leaking. What does Katherine think we are?"

"*You* are," the older man corrected. "She doesn't know I exist. Please. It will save my wrinkled old hide."

"Your hide is tougher than an elephant's."

"Not where Katherine is concerned. A man has his pride. I can't disappoint her. She'll find she is too old for you . . . me, but that is easier for me to deal with."

"Hell, yes, it's easier for you," Mike said. "Because I'm the one doing it."

Pembroke, satisfied she was appreciated, pulled away from the younger of her two masters and settled down on the hearth rug, her nose only an inch or two from Talbot's. Mike sighed. Pain was shooting through his arm. "Something clawed me in the dark on the tower stairs, and afterward I smelled the disgusting odor of sulphur. The woman can't be here at night."

"All right. She doesn't expect to stay here, anyway. I've told her how primitive our accommodations are."

Mike flexed his arm gingerly. "She won't realize what that means any more than I did before I came. It's only an illusion that the past is crumbling with these cracking walls. The past is so alive in the outer towers that sometimes I imagine I hear weeping or screaming."

Thomas swallowed. "Or the roars of the beast?"

"Yeah." Mike gazed thoughtfully at the floor before he pulled himself back to the problem at hand. "I don't like this plan of yours," he said in a flat, defeated voice.

"You're weaving a wicked and tangled web, Sir Thomas."

"Katherine can take care of herself," his father answered, chewing on the stem of an unlit pipe.

Mike gave in. He would honor his impulsive, ridiculous agreement, for his father's sake, but he hated it.

"She won't stay long," Michael, Sr., reassured him.

"How long, exactly?"

"She plans to be four weeks in Wales, but how much of that time she will spend here with us depends on . . . how pleasant her stay is."

"Depends on me, in other words." Mike's mood, made worse by his throbbing arm, was foul. "I can't put up with tripping over a lovesick spinster for a bloody month!"

The smile on his father's face was forced. "You'll come through it fine. You can carry on with your work, and I am here to play host when you're busy. Meantime, we've got some detective work to do—to find out who is sneaking around this crumbling old ruin playing dragon . . . and why. You'd better see a doctor about that arm."

"If anybody in the village got a look at these claw marks, it would really start something. We have to handle this ourselves, Dad. I disinfected my arm and my tetanus shots are up-to-date. We don't need panic, and we sure as hell don't need the people thinking we're crazier than they already think we are."

Thomas went to the little alcove that served as a kitchen. He took four eggs from a carton on the countertop and began breaking them into a bowl. The black-and-white dog raised his head and followed.

"We need more men," Thomas said. "This place is too big and too dark to find anything. Have you got a plan?"

"No, other than trying to follow the sulphur smell." The lights dimmed, brightened, and dimmed once again. "My immediate plan is to get to work on the generator." Tomorrow was Sunday, he thought, the one day the castle was at peace, without the shouts and bangs of the workmen. In spite of his impatience with the renovations, he welcomed Sundays.

Thomas had begun beating the eggs. "That's your whole plan? Follow the smell?"

"And arm myself in the gatehouse. I'll get him before he gets me." Mike pulled on a pair of boots and took a mackintosh from a hook by the door. "I don't know what your little old professor is in for once she gets to Aawn, Dad, but if the poor thing has fantasies about you...if she thinks she's going to meet a dragon slayer, she is going to get more than she bargained for."

"Just be nice to her," his father said in a fierce, deep growl. "Show her around, be polite and make sure she doesn't fall down the stairs. And introduce me as your father. I'll be your spunky, energetic father."

"I expect you to keep an eye on her and not let her go wandering off. I can't watch her every damn minute. I've got work to do. Come on, Pembroke, let's see what the weather is like out there."

Pembroke, tail wagging, joined her master as he ducked into the narrow, dark tower. The beam of his flashlight darted over the ancient stone walls. His voice seemed to fade into ghostlike echoes as he descended the winding stairs to the bottom of the castle's oldest tower—one of two towers that had stood firm through dark, misty centuries of constant siege. The outer towers and some of the passage walls had been rebuilt long ago, some as many as three times only to be ravaged again. Time had passed outside, but inside it felt to Mike as if every footstep that had ever fallen here—human or otherwise—could still be heard in the echoes of night.

HIS LAST LETTER CAME on a rainy day in May. It frightened her, but it was fear of the very best kind. That night, when rain was still slashing at her study window, she unfolded the letter again, under lamplight, and read it over.

"My dear Katherine, at last, after all these years, we will have a chance to meet...." Like always, he had written on thin, brittle paper with a heavy pen. "Your news was unexpected. I never imagined you would really come such a great distance, and I should like to believe it is I who lures you, but, alas, I know you well by now, Katherine dear. It is really he—the beast who claimed this lair long before me. However, while the dragon—bloody pest that he is—tries to frighten you away from this castle, I shall be doing my best to make you welcome."

Katherine smiled. Her gaze moved to a photo propped against the stem of her desk lamp. A man seated in a canoe on a rapidly running river, caught off guard by some unknown photographer as he adjusted his oars and glanced up. A handsome man with a mischievous smile and dark hair blowing in his eyes.

"Michael, you sound more like a Welshman than an American now. I don't know who you really are, but I like you...very much...." Dreamily, chin on palm, her shoulder-length auburn hair forming silky shadows on the desktop, she studied his photo. His wet, short-sleeved shirt, open in front, revealed a husky chest. Heavily muscled arms. Bare thighs showing over the rim of the canoe. His face wasn't very clear, but she could tell he was handsome. He'd never said when the photo was taken, but obviously it was quite a few years ago, before he'd moved to Britain. He looked to be in his late twenties or early thirties then. He would be in his fifties now.

What sort of man would choose to live in a haunted castle? *Her* sort of man! After four years of corresponding, she had learned that Michael Reese fascinated her more than any man she had ever known.

"Postscript," he had written hastily. "I don't want to frighten you, Katherine dear, but do be prepared—the dragon is here and very real. I have heard it breathing down the corridors and seen the shadows of its wings. And you will hate the smell of the bloody thing, which is one reason you will be glad you're not sleeping at the castle. There's nothing as bad as dragon's breath."

Was he trying to frighten her away, she wondered. Or get her so curious she couldn't stay away. Soon his musical words would be audible. Soon her mysterious man of letters would be close enough to touch. . . .

KATHERINE WELCOMED SPRING, this one more than any in a long time. Lilacs bloomed in the greening lawns of Allendale. Restlessness sprouted from every opening flower. The fragrance of lilacs signaled the closing of classroom doors and Katherine's freedom to leave—to become someone else. To become a woman no one in her hometown knew or would ever know—not even her sister.

It was exactly a mile from Katherine's town house to Rosalind's ostentatious home in the country club estates, making a pleasant morning walk. Pleasant, always, until she reached her sister's front yard—a grotesque zoo of animals that were not animals, trees cut in creature shapes—Rosalind's synthetic world.

Wearing crisp white shorts and white blouse with a yellow tulip embroidered on the pocket, and a wide-brimmed straw hat trimmed with yellow ribbon, Rosalind was kneeling on a cushion, carefully trimming a bush with shears.

"Good morning, Roz."

"Oh! Oh, Kathy! I didn't see you. Are you on foot?"

"It's a fine morning for a walk. What are you doing to that poor bush?"

Her sister stood up and examined her work. "Giving it character."

"Another of your crimes against nature. What's wrong with the character it already had. It looks like a vertical salamander now."

"What?" Rosalind set aside the shears and slowly pulled off her flowered cotton gloves. "Kath, love, the winter has been hard on you. You don't get enough oxygen in winter, cooped up in that airless classroom. Anyone could recognize this designer bush as a butterfly. Let's get you out of the sun."

"I hope the coffee's on."

"Of course. I was expecting you because the spring term was over yesterday. I said to Rusty this morning, it's that time when old Kath will be wriggling out of her cocoon."

In the spacious mauve-and-lavender designer kitchen, Katherine sat at the table in a windowed alcove that looked out on beds of spring flowers and asked, "Where are the kids?"

"At their Saturday piano lessons, followed by dance lessons." Rosalind carefully removed her hat and paused to examine her reflection in the glass of the built-in oven before she poured the coffee. She set two steaming lavender mugs on the glass tabletop and sat down. "New blouse?"

"I bought it for my trip."

Rosalind's smile vanished. "Your trip—your regularly scheduled disappearing act. Won't you stay around this summer? Just this once, the first summer Mother isn't with us? I have so many things going on— my garden club, my charities, all the kids' activities. During school vacation, the children are always underfoot. Won't you stay around and give me a hand this summer? I need you."

"You need a baby-sitter."

"That's not fair!"

"Roz, it's not fair to ask me to stay in Allendale to baby-sit. I have a life, too."

"What life?" Rosalind took a pearl comb from her hair and set it on the table. "What life are you talking about? Those secret summers? The whole town whispers about why you disappear the day Fielding College finishes spring term, not to be seen or heard from again until fall. It's truly bizarre, and I don't like it. I've never liked it."

Katherine stirred cream into her cup. "We've done this conversation to death. It's no particular concern of mine whether my life-style pleases anybody else or not."

"Your life-style causes me considerable embarrassment!"

Katherine fixed green-blue eyes on her sister. "Oh, come on, I have a shrub shaper for a sibling and you dare speak to *me* of embarrassment?"

"You won't be serious, will you? Or even kind. You know how proud I am of my topiary talents."

"Hey, Roz, this is me. For the sake of all the good citizens of Allendale, I'll go on faking an admiration for your deformed bushes and you'll go on pretending to guard my secrets. You have your shrubs and I have my summers. Who cares who cares?"

"I care who cares. I'm trying to maintain the social position expected of the Glenns . . . amid all the rumblings and whispers about my wandering sister."

Katherine was gazing at rainbows formed in the spray of the water sprinklers on the lawn. The sun felt warm through the window glass. Summer, the magic time for dreaming. . . .

"All right, Rozzie. This time I'll let you in on where I'm going. Bonnie at the travel agency will have it spread all over town, anyhow. I'm headed for Wales."

"Wales? Britain? Oh, my, yes! You've been doing all that research on British myths and medieval folklore lately."

"Lately? I've been doing that research for ten years."

Rosalind's eyes narrowed to tiny slits. Her finger began wagging in front of Katherine's nose. "Wait. Wales! A Welsh castle! You were writing to that eccentric American who bought a castle in Wales! Does he have something to do with this?"

"Absolutely. His castle is steeped in legend. A deathless dragon is believed to have lived in that old fortress for centuries. It is said to walk about the halls on moonless nights. Michael says all the local people still believe it, some claim to have seen it and he has heard it and smelled the thing. Fascinating, isn't it?"

Rosalind blew on her coffee. "Good lord, you've flipped! If your colleagues at Fielding get wind of this, they'll force you into retirement."

"Don't be ridiculous. I'm a *teacher* of medieval lore. This is a research project."

"Research. Umm. Who is this strange Michael who lives in a dragon's lair? You'd better watch it, Kath. What kind of nut would be sitting in a castle ruin smelling dragons?"

Katherine laughed. "He's hardly sitting. He's been working like a demon converting part of the castle into a hotel. And there are setbacks like his health. I think he left America because of health problems related to corporate stress."

"How did you hear about him?"

"I wrote to the town offices near the castle, because that dragon myth is so well-known. Someone there gave my letter to the new owner of the castle, and he wrote asking me what I knew about the legend. We've been corresponding ever since. We're . . . friends. Even exchanged photographs. He's handsome as well as rich, so I don't know why you're complaining."

"Handsome and rich?" Rosalind allowed her shoulders to relax slightly. "His own castle? Well . . . I suppose a woman would be a bit curious. How old is he?"

"Fifties. Judging from his photo and his general commentaries on life."

"Hmm. Ever married?"

"His wife is dead. But Roz, I'm not going over there because—"

"You'd better be. Good heavens, you'll be thirty-six in June! You're the town spinster by now."

"Not this again!"

Rosalind leaned close. "I'll be perfectly frank, my Kath. I've always believed your summers are spent in a clandestine thing with some well-known and very married man."

"You couldn't be more wrong."

Rosalind pulled a face. "I hate this coffee flavor. Orange rum crème they call it. Yuk, it's sickening." She pushed away the mug. "Of course it's a man. Why else would your seasonal whereabouts be kept secret?"

"Maybe my activities are not appropriate for a small-town college instructor."

"A nudist camp! I knew it! The tan!"

"Don't be ridiculous."

"What, then?" Rosalind took a drink from her cup, seemed to remember the orange rum crème and shuddered dramatically. "Please, Kath! I'm kin!"

"Would you like me to tell you I ride elephants in a circus?"

"I'd rather you told me the truth."

"What if I said that is the truth?"

The younger woman's lips quivered. "Why do you hate me?"

Katherine blinked. Her sister was on the verge of tears. She caught their reflections in the window glass—the auburn hair and pale eyes and small features—the close family resemblance between them. Katherine remembered two small girls sitting at their toy table with their dolls, serving sugar-water tea in tiny china cups, and the younger in tears when the lid of the teapot slid off and broke. She had tried to comfort her little sister. Roz had cared so much about that pink-and-white tea set with roses on the cups. She had been wrong and Roz was right; a sister deserved to be confided in. Now that their mother was gone, why hide the truth from Roz any longer?

Katherine drew a wallet from her handbag and sorted through it until she found what she was looking for. Rosalind picked up the photo and gasped. The figure in a silver sparkling leotard waving from the forehead of an elephant was Katherine.

"What? How did you get this?"

Katherine tossed out two more snapshots, which Rosalind studied in disbelief. Katherine, slim and beautiful in shimmering pink, standing on two bare-back horses. Katherine, sexy and sultry in black sequins and net stockings in the center of a circle of little dogs in hats.

"Oh, my God. Oh, my God! I'm struck speechless. This is you! This looks like . . . this is a circus! How did you get these pictures?"

"There are a lot more. Several summers' worth."

"I don't get it."

Katherine rose, emptied her mug of orange rum crème coffee into the sink and poured herself a glass of tap water. "You remember Tony—my fiancé in college?"

"I'd almost forgotten Tony. He's been dead a long time."

"It doesn't seem such a long time to me." She leaned an elbow on the counter. "Tony's family owned a circus. I never told you or Mother that, because I knew you'd hate it and object to my wanting to marry what you consider riffraff. The summer he was killed I was with his family's circus. I was there when the tent collapsed while we were trying to pull it in during a storm. I stayed on because his sister Gina and I were friends, and the family invited me back the next year, and the next. I started—" Katherine smiled. "I started helping train the dogs, and then the horses. You know how our good citizens of Allendale would react if anyone knew this, Rozzie. The college would fire me. And you'd be the butt of the jokes, right along with me. I thought it was kinder never to tell you. Until today. Until I realized you thought I didn't confide in you about my life because I didn't love you. I'm sorry. You did deserve to know, but could you have handled this when Mother was alive?"

Rosalind was staring at her, openmouthed. She eventually looked back at the pictures and began to laugh. "This is . . . It's true? You mean ever since Tony . . . your old Tony? You've been traveling with a circus? You? Understated Katherine with your dull gray business suits and your hair tied back and your lectures on history? I can't stand it! Look at you in this sparkling bathing suit! You're gorgeous! My sister is gorgeous! You fooled . . . everybody. . . . I'm hyperventilating! I'm going to die! I need water. . . ."

Katherine allowed herself to laugh over the expected reaction to her secret. Rosalind staggered to the sink, accepted the half-full glass of water from the circus performer and began to choke on her own laughter after one swallow. She grasped the counter for support.

"This is hysterical! Oh, Kath! If they knew! If people knew this . . ." She shivered with laughter.

"I had no idea you'd take it so well."

"Well?" Doubling over with laughter, Rosalind lost her hold on the counter. Her knees buckled. She grappled for Katherine's arm.

In unison they slid to the polished mauve tile floor, laughing as they had not laughed in years. Suddenly, magically, they had become young again, sisters again, playmates again.

"Crazy Kathy." Rosalind kept giggling. "Real elephants! And now a dragon?" She was lying flat on the floor on her back staring at the ceiling. "No, now a man! A strange and eccentric, possibly dangerous man you've never met!"

"I've met him, cautious Roz," Katherine insisted, leaning back against the dark oak cabinets, brushing tears of laughter from her cheeks. "I know him. He is literate bordering on literary. He's sophisticated and a gentleman. And quite frankly, he thinks I'm rather wonderful. He adores my photo, he said, and we're just...we're both fascinated with our friendship. With each other. Oh, yes, I do know Michael very well. I just haven't *seen* him yet."

2

THE CASTLE OF AAWN lay behind the brooding hills.
They could see no sign of it until the coach reached the
spot where the road bent toward a village called
Llanhafod, the moorlands opened and suddenly it was
there—a massive fortress rising out of the mist, its four
dark towers piercing a cold, slate-gray sky. Neither the
photos nor the fantasies had prepared Katherine for her
first sight of the Castle of Aawn. She gasped. Every one
of her five fellow passengers breathed sounds of awe.
Cameras began clicking around her.

The driver slowed the coach. Katherine rolled down
the window and felt the mist cold on her face. She
couldn't look away. They drew nearer and the fortress
grew larger as if it were moving toward her in the rolling of the mist. The massive, round-topped towers
buttressed high, hulking walls scalloped by battlements. The walls contained no windows and the towers but a few—if the narrow, elongated slits could be
called windows at all. The medieval fort was not welcoming; on the contrary, it had been constructed in the
dark centuries precisely to keep out enemies. Somehow, sometime long ago, a fiendish dragon had got in.
And never left.

The road followed a narrow, tumbling stream for a
time, until it curved and crossed over a rattling bridge.
At the crossing it forked with a rocky dirt road that
crawled up over a ridge in the direction of the castle. On

the ridge Aawn stood like a colossal stone monster against a cloudy shadow of lavender-green hills at its back.

The dragon's castle, she thought. According to legend, no one had ever spent three consecutive nights in its gatehouse, the tower built above the monster's cave. Anyone who dared stay a third night was never seen again, and red flames could be seen burning like torches in the windows of that tower. Even Michael did not sleep in the gatehouse tower. His rooms were in the keep.

"This is as close as we get this day," the driver said. "Excursions to the castle can be arranged in Llan-hafod."

The driver's voice brought Katherine abruptly back to the twentieth century. Aawn loomed before her, mysterious and real. She was almost there!

"Wait!" she said. "Please stop! I must get off here!"

The driver slowed to a halt and turned around. "But the village is over two miles away, miss, quite a long walk, and from the looks of the sky overhead, it's going to rain. The castle itself is farther than it looks. It's private property, the castle is, miss."

She felt the stares of her fellow passengers. "The man who lives in Aawn—Mr. Michael Reese—is a friend of mine. He was expecting me two days ago in the village, and since he can't be reached by phone I'll just walk on up there." She patted her tote bag. "I have an umbrella."

The driver got out of the coach. "Will you want me to take your bag to Mrs. Mills's house, then? I understand she, also, is expecting you."

"Yes, thank you. I'm sure I can get a ride to town. Please assure Mrs. Mills that I'll be there by evening."

Katherine stood on the wooden bridge and watched the coach move down into the shallow glen, leaving wisps of exhaust in its wake. As the engine drone faded, she was surrounded by the music of the wild land—the tumbling stream, wind in the high branches of trees that stood in clumps along the roadside. And in front of her rose the silhouette of Aawn—a castle oblivious to seasons and centuries.

Now under skies of a new age, the castle was frightening in its silence. "I'm really here!" Katherine told the wind. Heart pounding, welcoming the wet breeze in her face, she adjusted the strap of her shoulder bag and headed down the rough, narrow road. She was about to venture into the lair of a deathless, fire-breathing dragon. Even more exciting, it was the lair of a mysteriously fascinating man—her man of letters—the present lord of the castle.

The walk was a quarter mile, not more. A dark grove of trees to one side of the structure surrounded a small lake. When the road rose, she could see the reflections of the towers in the still, dark water. The scene looked like a painting, a backdrop for a film. Behind and beyond the castle the landscape lifted abruptly toward high, jagged hills. It was hard for Katherine to make the scene, or the moment, real. She had not anticipated the emotions the ominous ruin would stir in her. Although there was no sun, the castle cast a shadow. Moving into the coldness of that shadow, she shivered.

A wooden bridge, where once a drawbridge had been, crossed the moat, filled now with marshy runoff from the lake. There was enough water to please a pair of ducks, who moved lazily among the reeds. On each side of the bridge were two round tower bases, ruins of

the outer gatehouse. Katherine knew the layout well
from Michael's photographs and drawings. Stepping
over the bridge and into the grassy outer ward, she was
barely breathing.

She was surrounded by walls now, with more walls
in front of her, from which rose the enormous gatehouse tower, and to the side of it the great tower—the
keep. Behind, two drum towers and the crumbling
ruins of fortress walls were in various stages of dis-
repair. A bird shrieked from one of the drum towers;
otherwise, the silence was almost deafening. It was like
a time warp. The road had led her back into a darker,
more brutal century. Yet this was Michael's world. The
great towers looming before her were his home.

Gazing up at the massive keep, Katherine pictured
him sitting up there in the long northern nights like a
titled lord. In her vision he wore a heavy wool jacket
of dark brown plaid. He smoked a pipe that smelled of
rum while he read thick, yellowed books under a soft
lamp by the fire. And wrote letters to her.

Tire tracks had carved two paths across the outer
ward to the main gatehouse tower, which formed an
arch at ground level. The arch was the main entrance
to the castle. It led her through a passage, wide open
now, but once secured by the portcullis—an iron gate
hung on hinges from the top. Directly overhead were
stations where guards once stood ready to fling down
arrows. The gate passage opened into the bailey, the
inner ward—a wide expanse of green grass. On one side
was a garden, on another a clump of shade trees.

Trembling with excitement, with the gatehouse now
at her back, Katherine turned in a circle to gaze at the
castle proper. Four round towers connected by thick,
deep walls containing long passages and countless

chambers. Portions of the west and north walls and the two far towers were in ruin. But the large towers, the keep and the gatehouse, were remarkably well preserved.

Because Michael had written in such detail about the many workmen and the building going on, it was surprising to her that the bailey wasn't full of activity. Near the keep were piles of lumber and other building materials, covered with tarpaulins and plastic.

Suddenly Katherine was not alone. From out of the curtains of stone bounded a large black-and-white spaniel, his tail wagging furiously. The dog circled about her, wriggling with friendly greetings. Its eyes were soft and bright and welcoming.

"Where is everybody?" Katherine asked him. "Up there?" She raised her eyes to the keep that loomed above them and felt a cold, sweet sting of raindrops. The skies were spitting rain. A moment later it came down harder. She rushed for shelter, the dog running beside her.

They ducked into an archway that formed the entrance to the keep, and stood on a platform from which steps led both up and down. The dog looked up at her quizzically.

"Hey." She smiled at him. "You're the reception committee. You're supposed to be telling me where we're going."

Feeling the weight of the massive walls above and around her, Katherine reached out to touch the castle for the first time, as if only by touching could she be sure it was real. The stone was hideously cold. A sudden wind swirled and wailed through the arch.

Cautiously, grateful for the companionship of the dog, Katherine peered up the coiling tower stairs, into darkness punctured only by whiskers of light beaming through the arrow slits. Looking down, she could see only a well of blackness. Michael had written of the terrible dungeons below. Against the sound of rain softly splashing outside the arch came other sounds from somewhere inside the tower. There was banging, like hammering, and faint voices. A wagging tail beat against her leg. When she looked back at her black-and-white escort, she saw that he was holding a flashlight in his mouth.

"A mind-reading dog?" she said aloud, just before she noticed that in a corner of the stone foyer lay three more flashlights. The canine castle guard would have observed people taking flashlights countless times. "This is hospitality," she said, accepting the light. "Thanks."

Even with the light the stairway was treacherous. The dog climbed ahead of her. Katherine stepped with caution, one hand balancing against the cold wall. As she ascended, the voices and banging became louder. The beats of her heart became stronger. For four years she had wondered about this man, wanted to meet this man and now a few more steps . . .

Arrow slits shining in slants of hoary light marked the first landing. Here the dog paused and waited. Out of breath, Katherine caught up with him. She stood looking through a narrow archway into a spacious, high-ceilinged chamber that was filled with activity. Half a dozen men were at work, sawing, hammering, building. The smell of sawdust mingled with the dank, musty odor of the castle.

The light in this round room was a shock after the darkness. This would be the Great Hall, the largest chamber of the keep, where medieval banquets were held. At the far end stood a fireplace so large that several standing men could have fit inside it. In his letters Michael had written that the Great Hall was being converted into a lounge and dining room.

With all the noise and work going on, no one heard or saw her enter. Katherine took a few steps forward. One of the workmen, a powerful man wearing a sweat-soaked gray T-shirt and skintight faded jeans, with a bandage wrapped around his right arm, was working alone near one of the windows. The window recess was three feet above the floor and at least five feet deep—the thickness of the castle wall—and the man was attempting to climb into the recess, holding a thick pane of glass in a narrow wood frame. Wisps of rain were gusting in through the window, soaking the ledge. The stone was slippery, and he was obviously hampered by the injured arm. Swearing, he gave up trying to fit the pane into the window, and backed out of the recess. His knee skidded on the wet stone and, trying to balance the glass, he hit the injured arm hard against the wall. As Katherine drew nearer, the workman seemed to sense a presence behind him.

"Don't just stand there, you idiot! Can't you see the glass is slipping? Get a hold on this thing before the whole damn frame drops!"

Her swift reflexes had Katherine reaching around him and grabbing the frame, but it was too heavy, and she had to push forward with one knee to balance it.

"Why the hell were you just . . . ?" he began just before he looked down and saw the glitter of an opal ring on a slender feminine hand. His body went stiff.

"I can't hold this!" she grunted. "Do something!"

Recovering, he fell onto one knee and took the weight, and let it slide down his leg to the stone floor.

Once the glass frame was propped safely against the wall, he held his bandaged arm, grimacing.

Good lord, she thought at the first glimpse of his handsome face. *No one told me Welshmen looked like this*.

"You've . . . hurt your arm," she said softly.

He was staring at her so intensely Katherine took a step back and nearly tripped over the dog. What was the matter with him? Was he in so much pain he'd lost the ability to communicate?

More agonizing seconds prolonged his stunned stare. "Katherine?"

His voice was so deep and full it echoed in the hall. She blinked. "Yes, I'm Katherine. Michael Reese told you . . . he was expecting me?"

A smile, cautious at first, cracked his face. His confused eyes met hers. His hand finally extended toward her. "Katherine, welcome to Aawn. I'm Michael."

Her hand went to her forehead. "Michael?"

"What's the matter?" the deep voice was saying. "You look faint. Am I that disappointing?"

Michael? This youth who looked as if he had stepped out of a television commercial for a macho brand of beer? He was large and perfectly proportioned for his American-made jeans. His hair was thick and dark and his eyes were as blue as sky, and there was terrible mischief in his smile.

This wasn't possible! This wasn't Michael! Still, he did look like the photograph. She realized now, too late, that there had been no actual reason for her to assume that snapshot he had sent was several years old.

He was wiping wet sawdust from his hands onto the seat of his jeans. "You're two days late!"

She heard her own voice answering, "My plane was delayed and I missed a connection. I hope you didn't wait too long."

"I waited long enough to cause tongues to start wagging in the pub. How did you get here?"

"I asked the coach driver to drop me at the crossroad. I didn't want to . . . to go on by."

"You walked?"

"It isn't far."

He reached down to pet the black-and-white dog that was nuzzling at his leg. "I apologize for my language just now. The frame was slipping and I didn't realize it was you. . . ."

She smiled. "Of course you didn't. Is your arm badly hurt?"

He gave no sign of having heard her question. He was staring at her face as if he were in a kind of trance. When his eyes moved over her body, he tensed and blinked. It was obvious he had embarrassed himself, and this embarrassed her. "Your picture doesn't do you justice," he said stiffly.

"Neither does yours."

"Mine?" he asked.

"The snapshot you sent me."

"Oh, uh, yeah."

He can't be more than twenty-four, Katherine thought with sinking heart. How could she have made such a mistake?

The photo she'd sent of herself had been taken when she was seated at her desk in Fielding College. She wore a dark suit jacket in that photo, and a starched white blouse with pearls, and her reading glasses. Her hair had been pulled back at the neck by a black ribbon. He had been, after all, impressed by the fact that she was a scholar. He'd often said so.

Over the years the scholar had smiled privately at the thought of how horrified he'd be if she sent one of the photos of herself in sequins sitting on an elephant's head. He had seemed such a prude! A prude, and yet her friend Michael had been rather romantic in his letters. He, in his own way, was a scholar too, half poet, half scientist. He was so many things. But there had been no hint of . . . of *this* man! *How could this man be Michael?* It didn't make any sense!

His smile had become less mischievous, and melted into sincerity. "I apologize for my manners—for being unprepared. It's just that you're so much prettier than your picture. *Croeso i Gymru*, Katherine. In Wales that means welcome."

"Thank you, Michael."

"Well, hey, why are we standing here in the sawdust and all this pounding? What kind of welcome is this? Trumpets should be sounding and a feast laid out. Unfortunately all I can offer you is whiskey or French wine . . . in the questionable comfort of my upstairs apartment." He smiled warmly. "Come on, I'll lead."

She followed the beam of his flashlight on the tower stairs. The dog bounced up ahead of them. At the landing Michael paused in an archway and flicked on a lamp, muttering something about plans to wire the stairs for lights. They entered a semiround room furnished sparsely with wood and leather furniture. Tapestries hung on the stone walls, and there were both electric and kerosene lamps on the tables.

Katherine, still stunned over the shock of Michael's appearance, looked about in fascination. This, at least, was the way she had pictured it. The bookcase on one wall. A desk piled with blueprints and drawings of the castle renovations. A huge fireplace, with ashes on the grate. Deep shadows seemed to yawn and whisper as if something were hiding just out of sight. "This room is fabulous, Michael! Imagine a cozy apartment like this hidden in a bleak old tower."

"It's cold as hell in winter, I'll tell you. Always feels dank. I was claustrophobic for a long time because there are no decent windows. But then I told myself if my ancestors could stand it, I could, too. At least for a while. Eventually I plan to renovate a lower section that's more suitable for living." He motioned toward the sofa. "Sit down. Are you tired from your trip?"

"I don't know. I'm too excited to tell." She settled onto the cold leather seat and set her bag on the stone floor. "Michael, I thought I knew exactly what Aawn looked like, because of all the pictures and drawings you sent. But I *didn't* know. I didn't understand...."

He had been moving about the room, picking up books and papers from the floor. Now he stopped and looked at her. "Didn't understand what?"

"What it's like to be here...in here." Katherine hugged her arms as if she were cold. "This castle is so...sinister."

"It's the most sinister castle I've ever seen," he answered. "And I've seen quite a few. I've asked myself why and never found the full answer."

She gazed at his eyes. He gazed back, unblinking. She said slowly, carefully, "Aawn is haunted, isn't it?"

"You knew that before you came. Or didn't you believe it?"

"Not in the way I believe it now. There is a...a *feeling* here..."

He smiled, but not with enthusiasm. "The castle is at your disposal, Kathy. Explore all you want, except for just a few areas I'll point out that are too dangerous."

"What places are dangerous?"

"Here in the keep, the stairs between the top story and the ramparts are treacherous. We've installed a safety rope. And the dungeon level is too damned dark. Just promise you won't go wandering around in the dark. In the gatehouse, stay on the upper floors, don't go below ground level. And watch the steps of the ruins of the drum towers, especially the one on the south." He moved toward the kitchen. "What will you have to drink?"

"The wine, thanks. Michael, you sound over-cautious. I assure you I'm very surefooted. You needn't worry about me." Hearing the clink of glass from the kitchen, Katherine raised her voice so he could hear her. "Or by chance, are we talking about a different sort of danger? In your last letter you said something about there being more dragon activity in the castle."

"What did I write?"

"You don't remember what you wrote?"

Mike was back with two glasses and a bottle of red wine, which he poured with ceremony. His hand was unsteady. Perhaps his arm was hurting, she thought. He seemed unable to concentrate, and Katherine couldn't shake the feeling that meeting her was awkward for him. He was trying to conceal whatever it was that was bothering him.

"I hate to admit this," he said, "but I have a terrible memory. I don't remember what I wrote you...I mean...lately, about the dragon."

"You said you could smell its breath. That you sometimes heard its claws clicking on the stones. You said the thing is dangerous. I thought you were probably teasing, but it seemed so unlike you to tease about our dragon."

He handed her the glass and sat down with his own, in a chair across from her. "Our dragon, Kathy, is not a friendly beast, which you know from the legends. I wish I was teasing. I thought about trying to cover up everything, keep it from you, but then I was afraid if I did, you could get hurt. Something is slinking around the castle at night. Or someone."

She studied him, trying to digest what he was saying. "You sound almost . . . serious."

"I'm afraid I am."

"Then you weren't teasing in the letter! I wondered if you were trying to scare me away. Were you?"

"Maybe."

"Are you now?"

He gulped from his glass. The subject was making him even edgier. "Not scare you, just warn you. I wouldn't want anything to happen to you, Kathy."

He called her Kathy. In his letters he had never called her anything but Katherine. Definite proof that she was not the woman he expected. He must have pictured someone younger. But no, she'd told him her age. He had never mentioned his. Was it deliberate that he'd never mentioned his? Michael was interested in what she knew of the old legends, that was all. No young man like this man would be interested in a thirty-six-year-old spinster, except intellectually.

Why the hell had he led her on? He *had* led her on; a woman doesn't make mistakes about that. He'd even written some poems with romantic innuendos. Always in good taste, but now and then with unexpected daring. *Why would he do that?*

Katherine couldn't stop looking at him. The sight of the young man sitting across from her was unnerving at best. The muscles bulging under his T-shirt, his intense blue eyes, his sensuous smile stirred her feminine emotions the way a mixer stirred raw ingredients— whirring, pulling, twisting, with the sense that sooner or later the blend would all become one thick, sweet mixture. This man was not her fantasy—not her wonderful and mysterious man of letters! This Michael was a creature who stirred another side of her, one that she often feared because she had never come to terms with it. This youthful Michael was out of reach. He was one of life's cruel, ironic kicks.

"I sent someone into the village this morning to wait for you," the daydream across from her was saying.

"The coach driver will tell Mrs. Mills, where I am."

"Good. Telling Mrs. Mills anything is the same as telling the entire village. She's a good-hearted soul and the best cook in town, but she is also its eyes, ears and mouth. I think you'll be happy at her house, but be a little careful what you say."

Katherine met his eyes, even though it was not easy because their scrutiny of her was incessant. "Are you referring to the dragon?"

"Yeah. The village people claim to believe the dragon legend, but few really do. They're used to centuries of ghost stories. The men working out here have spread some rumors so some people are getting curious. And I'm getting nervous. I don't want the responsibility of having would-be dragon slayers constantly wandering through."

"I should think the stories would attract the tourists you want."

"Right. As long as they are just stories and nobody gets killed and eaten. I'd hate to have to explain it."

3

BEHIND HER from the doorway boomed a deep, raspy voice. "Blast this rain! But these trout are beauties, Mike! Once again Tywyllyn has given us our dinner."

A liver-and-white dog, like the spaniel Katherine had already met, except for its color, rushed in, came straight at Michael and eyed the stranger with friendly curiosity. Michael straightened but didn't rise from his chair. "The lady has arrived from America," he said.

Katherine turned. A man, white haired and white bearded, well into his sixties, set a pan of fish on the table and gazed at her as if she were an apparition.

"This is Katherine Glenn," Michael said. "Katherine, my father. His friends call him Thomas."

Thomas Reese blinked, then finally smiled. "Welcome to Aawn! I apologize that I can't shake your hand, Katherine. I've just come from cleaning fish. How did you get here? I was on the lakeshore and I didn't see a car, didn't hear any barking. Well, no matter, here you are. So! You've come all this way to see our crumbling ruin! Mike tells me our resident dragon lured you."

How incredibly strange, Katherine thought, that Michael had never mentioned his father was here. Thomas Reese must have only recently arrived.

"Yes, your dragon lured me," she answered. *And your capricious son lured me and I'm not sure why.* "And from what I've seen, there is enchantment in every pore of this castle."

Thomas Reese's watery blue eyes fixed on hers. "My dear, if in murky ages past any of that magic ever left Aawn, I think you have brought it back. But excuse me a moment, will you, while I put the fish on ice and wash my hands?"

Katherine reached for her glass. The old man was as eloquent in his speech as Michael had been in his letters. "How long has your father been here?"

"Uh . . ." He called toward the kitchen. "How long have you been here, Dad?"

There was a pause before Thomas answered, "Lord, I've lost track of the weeks. One does. Time stands still here. It's several months now. I came to see Mike, Katherine, and I fell under the spell of the place."

Thomas returned to the sitting room and poured himself a glass of whiskey. "This castle is more demanding than a whining spouse, let me tell you. Her needs are endless. We lay pipes and floorboards and plaster in our sleep. Are you cold, Katherine? Blasted cold rain coming down out there. Chills one to the bone. Build a fire for our guest, Mike."

His son knelt in front of the fireplace, throwing on kindling and a log from the supply that was stacked on the hearth. "Hope the smell of wet dog doesn't bother you, Kathy. This wet ball of fur, by the way, is Pembroke."

"And that's Talbot," Thomas said, handing back her filled glass and nodding toward the black-and-white dog. "Purebred English spaniels. The breed has been a tradition at the castle for generations. Talbot takes his duties seriously as a castle guard, but I'm afraid Pembroke prefers chasing rabbits across the hills and scaring up frogs along the shore. Have you just arrived? Has Mike shown you around?"

"I just came," she answered. "And interrupted his work, for which I apologize. I don't want to be a bother." Her polite calmness was fraudulent. Katherine was aching to walk the passages of the ancient fortress, to listen to its whispers and its screams, to feel the vibrations of the spirits who had once breathed here, and died here.

Michael didn't seem to understand that she had fallen in love with Aawn long before she saw it. How could he not know this from her letters? How could he not know that in much the same way she had fallen in love with him, too? The castle, for all its fearful mysteries, felt almost like an old friend. But Michael was a stranger.

He seemed kind, though. His stares were baffling but not unkind. Both her hosts were making her feel welcome. In her million fantasies about her first hour in this tower, Katherine had seen the stone walls and the great fireplace blazing. Michael in wool and suede, showing her the architect's drawings and his precious old books.

The reality, however . . . The smell of dog, which she didn't mind, was not the same as a gentleman's cologne. Michael's handsome, aging father was a complete surprise. The ripple of muscles on Michael's husky arms and under his T-shirt across his wide expanse of chest. His skintight jeans and the thick mat of his dark, slightly curly hair. Katherine was sick with disappointment and trying desperately not to show it. She wanted *her* Michael.

"We have fresh trout for dinner," Thomas was saying. "You'll stay, of course."

"I haven't been into the village yet. Since it's so close, I'd hoped to beg a ride to Mrs. Mills's house. She plans on me for dinner tonight. If I could, I'd love a rain check."

"Of course. Though you're going to discover my cooking can't compete with Mrs. Mills's."

Michael removed dry grass from under Pembroke's collar and tossed it into the fire. "I have no complaints about your cooking, Dad. It's interesting how our values change. If anybody had ever told us we'd be cooking and hauling water up these blessed—"

"We don't always have to haul water up," the older man interrupted. "Sometimes the pumping system works. Sometimes the generator works. God smiles, it's working now. Sometimes it stops raining . . . and the hills are covered with flowers."

Katherine smiled. "I envy you both."

"Why?" Michael asked.

"You have the courage to live a dream. This castle is far more dream than real, in this century. You have the courage to turn it all into a purpose . . . a livelihood."

"Courage isn't the proper word," Thomas said. "Madness better describes it."

Michael rose. "Madness is what we left behind. Do you want to see the rest of the keep, Kathy? Or would you rather wait until the workmen leave? The noise ruins the atmosphere, and the atmosphere is the main thing."

"I'll wait. You probably want to get back to that windowpane. I hope your arm is okay."

Thomas had begun the lengthy process of lighting his pipe. He stopped, holding the pipe in midair. "Is that arm giving you problems?"

"It's just slowing me down is all. I didn't thank you for your fast footwork, Kathy. I'd have dropped that glass if you hadn't been there."

"Maybe you ought to put me to work. I learn fast, and I'm used to working with my hands."

"Good heavens!" Thomas blurted. "At Aawn we don't submit guests to labor!"

"Especially not our first and most distinguished guest." The son cast the father a strange, uninterpretable glance. Michael was gulping wine ferociously. Katherine had already lost count whether this was his third or fourth glass. His self-assured manner had been interrupted time and again by moments of uncertainty, nervousness. Her presence made him so nervous he wasn't able to conceal his unease.

"I enjoy work," she said in defiance. And she wondered why, when she'd been writing to him for four years, it had been only in the past few months that Michael had written about the massive renovations. From the little she had observed, the work probably hadn't been going on any longer than a few months. Why not before? Red tape? Financial reasons? Or was it the illness he had mentioned and then refused to discuss . . . like he refused to discuss that bandaged arm?

As if he read her thoughts, Thomas asked, "Mike, are you in pain?"

"You ought to know." He sat down in the chair again, leaned back and closed his eyes.

Katherine said, "You don't seem to feel well. Perhaps when the workmen leave I could ride into town with them."

His eyes remained closed. "Nonsense. I'm your escort here. I'll drive you in. It only takes ten minutes. No bother at all. I'm fine. Have some more wine. I'm ahead of you."

The older man was puffing heartily on his pipe by now. "There's a lot to see, Katherine. But drat this rain!

Too much of the ruin is exposed to the elements. It's a bad day for anything but enjoying the wine and the fire."

"Michael was very busy before I came."

"Michael has taken the rest of the day off," Michael said. "It's a major occasion. The day Katherine has become flesh and blood." He opened his eyes. "She doesn't look like her picture, does she, Dad?"

"Well not exactly, no."

"Of course I do," she said.

"Nope. Not a damn bit. You're a complete surprise." He grimaced. "Someday you're going to hate me."

A stiff silence separated them. Katherine keenly felt the disconnection. "What do you mean I'm going to hate you?"

His father cleared his throat. Michael shrugged and said, "Pay no attention to me. I'm a clod."

What was the matter with him, she wondered. The wine? Or was the man a little crazy? Something odd was going on.

She said, "You, Michael dear, are the surprise."

"Me? Why?"

How could he not know? "Well, let's just say you are different in flesh than in blue airmail envelopes."

"Isn't everyone?" He leaned forward to pour more wine. "I mean, who is really himself on paper? We are all someone else on paper. Hell, you could have been a little old lady for all I knew. Right, Dad? I had no way of knowing she was a beautiful woman. No one told me that."

"Mike," his father said. "What I suggest—provided you remain sober enough to drive—is that when you drive Katherine into Llanhafod you stop off at the hospital."

"What for? Oh, hell, we've covered this. No doctor."

She looked from one man to the other. "What is it? What's wrong?"

"Nothing serious," Michael answered. "I hurt my arm several days ago and it has become infected."

"You have been favoring that arm. I've been watching you. Surely you ought to have it looked at."

"Nah. It's all right."

"Don't be a fool," Thomas said. "You have to get your priorities in order. You're going into town soon, anyway."

"Can I have a look at it?" Katherine asked. "I've had experience with first aid. I know something about infections."

Michael looked doubtful. "Infections at the college?"

"I spend my summers traveling with a group of performers. I'm the appointed medic and I know what I'm doing. If the infection isn't too bad, I can treat it. If it's to the point of needing emergency medical treatment, I can tell. Why are you so stubborn about it?"

He glanced at his father, then back at her. "It's an ugly wound. I'd never subject you to such a thing."

"Maybe you'd better," Thomas said. "Katherine is not going to spread any gossip. Now that I've—we've met her, I see she's not the fragile person you led me to believe she was. Anyway, I think she deserves to know what's been going on around here, for her own safety."

"Fragile?" she muttered, staring at Mike, challenging him.

He was not looking at her, but at his father. Finally, his broad shoulders sagged. "I'm taking you at your word about this medic thing. If you faint, it will kill my arm trying to catch you."

Katherine pulled a face, reached for his arm and began gently loosening the tape. "How did you get hurt?"

Neither man answered. The room became deadly silent except for the eerie popping of the fire. Uneasiness quivered in her stomach while she unwrapped his arm. There was not one wound, but three. Scabbed over, but red and swollen around the dark red slashes. Her heart began pounding.

"These wounds!" she breathed, sucking in air and almost choking. "These look like gashes from a giant claw!"

Katherine's eyes darted from one man to the other.

"How did you get hurt?" she repeated in a grave, commanding voice that didn't seem her own. Michael had remarked that it would be a mistake to go to the village hospital for treatment of these wounds. A mistake?

Mike answered hesitantly. "I suppose you need to know if you're going to be exploring around the castle. The truth is, I was attacked in the dark by someone I couldn't see."

"Someone or something," Thomas interjected.

Katherine reeled. "Something attacked you...in the dark?"

"The smell of sulphur was strong in the gatehouse that night and I went down to the bottom to investigate. It had happened before—that smell and odd sounds down there, but I'd never found anything. This particular night something spooked the dog and knocked my flashlight out of my hand and slashed me. Talbot jumped at it, even made contact, I think, but he decided to stay with me rather than pursue. The dogs can't stand the sulphur smell. I heard a weird sound like wind in a tunnel and an echo of a clicking down the passage, and then nothing more. Old Talbot found my flashlight. He has this thing about flashlights. When I turned it on I saw blood all over the floor. The dog's footprints and mine were in the blood, but no other."

She stared at him, her eyes filled with horror.

Mike clenched his fist. "Hell, Kathy, you asked. I didn't want to tell you, but I'll concede you need to know why it's risky to be in the deeper areas of the castle."

Her words came in unsure breaths. "You wrote about the smell and the sounds like flapping wings and clicking claws. I thought you meant they were sort of...sort of imaginings, like ghosts...subtle and barely there, like things some people might see while others don't."

"You mean a normal haunting."

She sucked in air. "Just what, exactly, is a *normal* haunting, Michael?"

"What you just described. Sounds and smells and shadows lurking in corners. Ghosts that no one can prove are there because some see them and some don't. My arm is proof that there is something in this castle besides a vaporous spirit. This thing is vicious, and its antics are getting out of hand."

Examining his arm, she said weakly, "Very much out of hand. These wounds are deep. You need antibiotics to fight the infection."

"How will I explain it at the hospital?" He winced when she pressed the skin between the slashes.

"It hurts badly, doesn't it?"

"Yeah."

Katherine reached into her handbag for her glasses and put them on for a closer look. "I could disinfect the wounds, but it wouldn't be effective enough because the infection is too advanced. Your arm feels hot. Do you see this small red streak? And this one? These are danger signs. You haven't a choice, Michael. You need a doctor for this. If I were you, I wouldn't put it off another hour."

He twisted the arm to get a better look at it. "Those streaks weren't there this morning."

"Your arm feels hot?" Thomas asked. "You'd better listen to the lady, even at a risk to our peace. If the hospital staff asks what happened, make up a plausible story."

"Like what? The kittens have grown too big to play with?"

Katherine shrugged. "They can't refute what you say."

"If they tell I'm lying, it'll start a wave of whispers. The dragon of Aawn is an accepted resident of this valley. People believe the old beast has been pretty quiet since the days when he ate people on a regular basis, but legend says he'll get restless again."

"It looks as though he has. But dragon or not," Katherine said, "if you don't get yourself a strong dose of antibiotics and a tetanus booster, you could be in trouble."

She replaced the bandage carefully while he sulked. "Who would attack you in the gatehouse? Honestly, if I wasn't *looking* at this, I'd think you were playing games with me."

"No, someone is playing games with *me*," he answered, "and I don't like it. I'll find out what attacked me no matter what it takes." He sighed heavily. "This is no good. You just got here. I don't want to rush you off so soon."

"Don't be silly. It's not as though I weren't coming back tomorrow. I'll check in with Mrs. Mills. I think we ought to go right now."

Rising from his chair, Thomas said, "Already the dragon is interfering with your visit. Cursed beast."

"Surely," she said, "you don't really believe any animal could have done this?"

Thomas's pale eyes were somber. "Dragons don't exist, but something is certainly acting like one."

"It's so bizarre!" *I fell asleep on the plane over the Atlantic Ocean and I'm only dreaming this,* she thought. *The dragon can't be real, and neither can this handsome hunk who claims to be my Michael but in no way resembles him....*

Mike disappeared for a few moments and came back buttoning the cuffs of a long-sleeved shirt. He slid into a rainproof windbreaker. "You and the red streaks have got my attention," he said. "Let's get this over with."

At the doorway he reached for her hand. "Better hang on to me until you get used to the tower stairs and know where the damaged steps are. It's a hell of a drop to the bottom."

His hand was warm and firm. She felt the protective strength in the touch of a stranger. This was the castle he described, but even more desolate than he described, more lonely, because her friend was not here.

The enchanted castle drew her. On some level of her being, she felt at home. Lonely, yet at home. Enthralled, yet disappointed. These were conflicting sensations of someone too tired to think, she told herself as she descended the winding tower stairs grasping tightly to the hand of a young man who bore wounds that looked for all the world like the claw marks of the castle's resident dragon.

HIS TRUCK BUMPED over the muddy roads. Rain splashed on the windshield and the wipers sang an elvish song.

Katherine asked, "You wouldn't have put off seeing a doctor, would you? I mean, you'd have realized the infection was bad."

"I suppose so. The sawdust doesn't help."

"How are you feeling otherwise? The shock of this horrid attack couldn't have helped your heart any."

"My heart?"

"I'm sorry to bring up your health. It just slipped out. I was very concerned about you when you were hospitalized last year. I suppose I only assumed it was your heart, from what you wrote. Such a trauma as a physical assault like this would really shock one's system."

"My system is fine." Michael gritted his teeth and added softly, "I assure you, I don't have a heart problem."

"That's good," she said, unsure whether or not she believed him because the very mention of last winter's illness was causing him discomfort. "Certainly, you're looking fine. It must be the wonderful Welsh country air."

"Yeah, the air . . ." he muttered in a flat, tight voice.

Katherine glanced over at the man who was twisting the wheel to avoid a washed-out portion of the narrow road. Her mention of his health bothered him. His type didn't like to appear vulnerable. It could have been a bout of pneumonia for all she knew because he had talked about how cold the castle was in winter. He had been worried, though, at the time, and said so in a letter. It was hard to imagine this man sitting at his desk writing those letters . . . about his illness or anything else.

Except maybe about the dragon.

"Your father is a lovely man, but a surprise. You never mentioned that your father was living at Aawn."

"Didn't I? Oh, yeah, he's . . . there."

"Michael, is something wrong? You seem awfully uncomfortable. Are you feeling all right?"

"Maybe I'm a little feverish."

"The infection? Good heavens, I hope not!" She reached over to touch his forehead. "You don't feel feverish."

"I think I'm starting to. I'm not at my . . . uh . . . at my best today, for which I apologize. You must be exhausted from your long trip." The truck hit a bump and he shifted into second gear.

"I think the fatigue is starting to kick in." She studied him. "Your arm is hurting every time you shift, isn't it? Would you like me to drive?"

"It takes more strength than most women have to shift this hunk of junk. I'll manage." He smiled at her. "I doubt I could stand the trauma of watching you try to adjust to driving on the left side of the road."

"What left side? We're going right down the middle."

"Not to worry. I'll get us there in five more minutes."

She listened to the rhythm of the wipers. Outside, the green hillsides were dotted with grazing sheep. Watching one scamper up the hill, Katherine squinted and sat forward. "Those sheep have long, bushy tails!"

"Welsh mountain sheep," he said.

She scanned the hillside. "And those, Michael! Some are all black except for their long white tails! How strange they look. They wag their tails like dogs."

"They'll all come home wagging their tails behind them," he sang.

"I'm surprised you never wrote me about the mountain sheep's tails."

"Hmm. So fascinating a subject overlooked. Surely I had better things to write about. Didn't I?"

She cocked her head. "Oh, I don't know. Perhaps." Katherine sighed. She turned away from the scenery outside the rain-streaked window. "Michael, what do you think attacked you in the castle?"

"I figure it had to be a man armed with a weapon like a three-pronged garden hand rake."

"And the sulphur smell? And the noises?"

"Legend says these have always been in the castle. Certainly they have been since I came. But lately I think these are simulated by somebody. The smell is too strong. The noises are too loud. But why anybody would go to that kind of trouble, I can't fathom."

"Do the local people resent you buying the castle?"

"Some might. But as many others welcome our restoration efforts. A hotel will bring revenue to the village. I've gone over this in my mind, trying to think of a motive for anybody to want me out of Aawn. I draw a blank."

"But someone does," she said.

"Yeah. It looks like someone does."

Katherine gazed over at him. "How can you sound so casual about such a thing? Such an unbelievable thing?"

"I'm trying not to alarm you any more than necessary."

"Why should I not be as alarmed as you?"

This seemed to throw him. "I...have to protect you."

Katherine smiled. "I see. There is danger in the castle. The legend has come to life. And you are the knight who must slay the dragon to protect—"

Michael finished the thought for her "To protect his lady."

Somewhere, sometime, she had heard those words before. Katherine shivered, because his words were of the past. What magic here, she wondered, could make anyone believe in fairy tales? Her literary gentleman was transformed into a knight. And she his lady.

What kind of craziness had she walked into?

4

GRAY SLATE ROOFS of the village protruded from their nest of greenery. The buildings, all white save for the high, square stone church tower, seemed to form no pattern. On approach, short, curving streets came into view.

A bridge over a lively stream led them to the main street. It was a wide street with shops along each side. Colorful signs hung above the little stores. The bakery, butcher, confectioner's shop, ready-to-wear wool clothing, a greengrocer, a real-estate agency. Many of the buildings were patterned in black and white, English style, and none was more than two stories high. There were white wooden shutters at the upper windows, and on this summer day, even with the intermittent rain, all the shutters were open. The gray stone bell tower of the church loomed over the town as it had done for some four hundred years.

"It's a lovely village—and just as you described it in your letters." She looked hard at him. "You never called me Kathy in your letters."

The truck slowed to a crawl. "That's because I hadn't seen you. Now I know that Kathy suits you better. And Mike suits me better than Michael."

"Why do you sign letters Michael? You were being formal in the beginning, I suppose. I agree, Mike suits you better."

"You say that strangely. I'm not what you expected."

"Not at all."

She saw him tense slightly. "Are you disappointed?"

Katherine hesitated.

He asked quickly, "What about me disappoints you?"

She tried unsuccessfully to smile. "I just . . . had the impression you were older."

They were in the heart of the village now, midway down the only commercial thoroughfare. There was little traffic, but several people were on the street. Shop doors were open; it was a business day. Michael stopped for a pedestrian crossing in front of the car. "I'm older than I look."

So am I, Katherine thought, not wanting to say it aloud.

In the span of three minutes they had passed through the city center. He turned onto a side street and drew up to the curb in front of a small two-story house with a "B and B" sign posted in front. "Your accommodation, my lady."

"Thank you." She paused before opening the truck door. "You're on your way to a doctor, then?"

"To the hospital. There's always a doctor on call."

He got out and came around to open the door for her, and took her satchel from the back. "Don't mention to Mrs. Mills that I'm on my way to the hospital. It's best to ignore any subject that you don't want broadcast all over town."

The house sat only a few meters in from the curb. Under front windows a low wire fence protected a bed where summer flowers were blooming. Net curtains hung in the windows.

Mike looked at his watch. "You're in time for dinner. I'll pick you up here tomorrow morning. I'm sure you'll want to sleep late, so what time is good? Around eleven?"

"I planned to find some transportation of my own so you wouldn't have to—"

"It's no bother. The town is so close."

He opened the door without knocking. Approaching from the inner hall was a rotund woman wearing a dark wool skirt and a pink sweater. Gray curls wisped around her pleasant oval face. Smiling broadly, she extended her hand.

"Mike Reese! Sure, I was expecting you to deliver my guest to me before time for tea."

"We were delayed. Mrs. Mills, this is Katherine Glenn."

"Katherine, welcome. I received the message from the coach driver that you stopped to visit the castle. He told me you were acquainted with the lad here."

"Katherine and I are old friends," he said. "She knew I'd be worried about her late arrival."

The woman's eyes moved curiously from Katherine to Michael. Katherine found herself holding her breath, wondering what thoughts were behind the wise, dark eyes.

Mrs. Mills's smile seemed permanent. "Michael, lad, will you stay and have dinner with us this evening?"

"Thanks, I can't. Too many errands to take care of. But I hope the invitation stands." He reached for the door. "See you tomorrow, Katherine." His eyes lingered on hers, hesitating just long enough to make her feel the same discomfort she had felt in the tower, sitting across from him unable to stop herself from admiring the sheer beauty of him. Animal magnetism she had heard it called. Michael had a sexiness about him that put her on edge whenever he got close enough for her to be pulled into its magnetic field. Worse, he seemed to sense it.

"Tomorrow," he repeated huskily, as if the word *tomorrow* had a hundred secret meanings. He set her small bag down, and he was gone.

"The lad never stops," Mrs. Mills said. "Works night and day, he does. But I admire an ambitious man. Here, come in. I'll show you to your room so you can freshen up before dinner if you like." She started up the stairs. "What did you think of Aawn? It's sturdily built, they say, as castles go, particularly the keep. The two oldest towers were never damaged in a siege for mysterious reasons we'll never know. Legend says the dragon was the reason, that the castle is enchanted."

She turned right at the top of the steps and opened one of the three doors. Katherine entered a pleasant room painted in shades of rose and pink. Two single beds were spread with matching flowered comforters. There were linen covers on the dresser tops and paintings in pastels on the walls. Her bags, brought in by the tour coach driver, were placed next to a mahogany wardrobe in one corner. Outside was a view of the green velvet hills and grazing sheep, and beyond the hills rose a ridge of mountains that formed a backdrop for the ominous towers of Aawn. The lake at the foot of the towers was a shine of silver in the lingering summer-evening sun.

The fatigue of the journey and the emotional overload of her first hour at Aawn caught up with her suddenly, like a cloud swooping down and wrapping her body in cotton.

"I'm afraid I'll have to skip dinner," she told her landlady. "I'm suffering jet lag from so many hours on the plane and the delays and the ride all the way out from Manchester. I doubt if I could stay awake another hour."

Mrs. Mills smiled. "Very well. You'll be hungry for a fine breakfast, then, by morning. Is nine o'clock too early?"

"Oh, no, not if I go to bed now."

"The W.C. and the bath are marked. I hope you'll be comfortable. Anything you need, let me know. Most of my guests are tourists who come in just for a day or two. It's lovely to have a weekly guest and someone genuinely interested in our local history. Aawn castle was built around the time of the Edwardian castles, I believe."

Aawn was built after those of Edward, Katherine might have corrected, and didn't. The woman's words were coming off and on like a radio fade-out. Barely able to force herself to listen, she sat down on the bench of the dormer window.

"Well. Have a fine rest," the woman said in her thick Welsh accent. "And again, a warm welcome to you." She closed the door quietly when she left.

Fifteen minutes later Katherine was showered and in bed, staring at a high, cream-colored ceiling that showed cracks of age through many layers of paint. Sleep didn't come so easily, after all. Her swirling thoughts wouldn't settle.

Michael. Who the devil was he? Certainly not the man she thought she had come to know during their four years of correspondence.

In the beginning he had been interested only in the legend of his castle and its history. But as time went by they began to write of other things. She wrote of her research projects and of books she had read, of the dance recitals of her little nieces, and winter nights by the fire grading students' papers or watching a movie on the VCR. He wrote of the changing seasons and of migrating birds, and the gulls that ventured inland from the sea and found his little lake. He wrote of lonely nights by the fire, winter nights when he was surrounded by ice-cold walls of stone. He wrote of the bramble bushes that grew along the low stone fences in the countryside, and the wild daisies on the moorlands.

They had seemed so alike, the two of them. Quiet, studious people, not inclined toward an active social life. Katherine had never shared the other side of herself with Michael because she had assumed he wouldn't relate to it. Maybe it served her right to be so surprised by him. It was pretty hard to blame someone for not disclosing his total self when she had done the same.

She was wrong not to write about the circus world that had meant so much to her. She should have shared her love for it—the smells of dust and straw and musty canvas and the sounds of tigers' roars and elephants' honks and excited shouts of children. Had she given the man more hints of the younger side of herself, he would surely have done the same. They had been playing some stupid game, sharing only what each imagined the other wanted to hear. Sharing only what they knew they had in common. As if there was nothing else.

Michael had looked utterly stunned when he saw her. Why? What had he expected? And he! He was so young!

How could she have made such a monumental mistake? The man and his letters didn't match. The way he spoke didn't match the way he wrote. Had she created something in her mind that didn't exist, or had he deliberately misled her? She was greatly bothered by the possibility that he had.

He knew she was an unmarried woman many years his senior. Why had he seemed so fascinated with her and flirtatiously called her "my Katherine?" She wasn't "my Katherine" now. All of a sudden she was Kathy.

Nothing was right—nothing except Michael's eyes when he was caught off guard staring at her. They were eyes that seemed to know secrets about her and probed for more. Sensual reminders of the words that had teased her sometimes on pages of letters read deep in the night. The comment he had made in the truck about the knight and his lady was something the old Michael might have said in his letters, caught up in the romantic lore they both loved. His words had set her heart to fluttering.

As the shadows deepened in her room, Katherine sighed. It was not going to be the summer she had envisioned in her thousand daydreams. Eyes filling with tears, sick with disappointment, she tried to force herself to slide into the down of sleep. Katherine all but wept in the gray silence.

What a letdown. And on top of everything else, some foul-smelling creature that flew along dank castle halls at night was trying to kill him. . . .

BREAKFAST WAS OVER BY TEN, which left Katherine an hour to acquaint herself with the little village of Llanhafod before Mike picked her up. The morning was crisp and still. Clouds were gathered in pockets across the expanse of British sky. Between the gray clouds the sun shone brightly. She walked the sidewalks of Centre Street, gazing into shop windows and listening to the musical lilt of Welsh voices. And thinking about Michael Reese.

Mike's wife had died before he came to Wales, he'd written. A widower at such a young age? He couldn't have been over twenty when he bought the castle four years ago, so his wife must have been a teenager! He had never talked about her in his letters, or anything much about his past. How could he? He wasn't old enough to *have* a past.

She stepped into a small shop that displayed postcards on a tall, turning rack. Roz would be waiting for a postcard with a report of first impressions. *Not on your life, Roz!* she thought. *This one you wouldn't believe!* If Roz were ever to see a photo of Mike Reese, the teasing would never stop. He looked as if he belonged on a magazine centerfold.

The clerk, a freckled girl, smiled from behind the counter. "Good morning."

"Good morning." Katherine took her seven postcards—three of which were of the local castle—to the cashier.

"Were you there yesterday?" the girl asked, glancing at the cards. "At the castle?"

"Yes, for a short while."

"You're American. Are you the friend of Mike Reese?"

"Yes." Katherine smiled. "But how could you know?"

"Gossip travels like wind around here. Mike brought you into town yesterday. Since there are no scheduled tourist visits to Aawn at the moment, it stands to reason you must be a friend. That'll be a pound ten."

Again the forward questions, and from a stranger. Katherine was stunned. All right, the game could go two ways; a stranger could fish for information, also. She asked, "Is Mike a friend of yours?"

"In a way," the girl answered. "Everybody knows him, of course."

"Of course?"

"He rather stands out, him being an American and a bachelor and, well...you know." When she looked away, the girl was blushing.

I guess I do know, she thought. *Damn it.*

"People tease him about being the castle lord," the girl volunteered.

Katherine picked up her small bag. "Does being the castle lord have something to do with everyone's...interest in Mike?"

"Of course. People keep an eye on him." The girl leaned forward and wrinkled her nose. "I should say, some people do. I'm happy to welcome you to Llanhafod if you're a friend of Mike's. My name is Cadi Morgan."

"Katherine Glenn." She looked at her watch. Mike would be at the house soon to pick her up, and Cadi Morgan would no doubt hear about it within the hour. Mike was noticed in the village, all right. By the women.

MRS. MILLS WAS DUSTING the front parlor. Choir music was playing on the stereo. Katherine paused in the doorway. "Do you know where I might rent a bicycle?"

The woman ceased her work. "I'm sure I could find you a bicycle. When do you need it?"

"Tomorrow. I have a ride today, but I don't want Mike to feel obligated to chauffeur me. I'd enjoy biking."

"I'll ask around. Were you in the village just now?"

"For a stroll, yes. I met Cadi Morgan, who knew I came to town with Mike yesterday."

Mrs. Mills laughed, raised her feather duster and resumed her work. "Cadi is only one of several eligible lasses in town. You'll know it soon enough—they all have their pretty heads cocked in the direction of your friend Michael."

"I was beginning to suspect as much."

"One can't blame them, now, can one?"

Katherine leaned against the door frame. "And how does Mike take to the idea of being ... quarry? Does he play the village squire? Has any girl won the lord's favor?"

"Ah, no. A bit standoffish, he is. There's gossip he's been married before. Has he?"

Katherine straightened. "He doesn't talk about his past," she said carefully.

"For certain, but all the same, I thought...you being an old friend ..."

Katherine turned toward the window. "The truck is pulling up now," she interrupted. "I'm invited to dinner at the castle tonight, so I won't be back until rather late."

This would get around town, too, but it couldn't be helped. Adjusting the strap of her shoulder bag, she hurried out.

It was Thomas, not Mike, who came around to open the door for her, apologizing for the truck and telling her she looked lovely this morning. Dressed in tweed and leather, Thomas Reese was a gentleman of class— the sort of man she thought she was going to meet.

"Mike has been at work on the windows since dawn," Thomas said as they drove through the village streets.

"How is his arm?"

"Under medical scrutiny. He has to make a run back this afternoon for another injection. I don't worry about Mike when he complains, only when he doesn't. He'll be all right—he was complaining loudly this morning."

"Won't working make the arm hurt more?"

"Wouldn't stop him, even if it did. The lad is obsessive. Works sometimes fifteen or sixteen hours a day, seven days a week."

Through the open window Katherine breathed in the fragrant air of the summer morning. "It must have been difficult for him, then, during his illness, those long weeks when he couldn't work."

A troubled expression clouded Thomas's face. He swallowed with discomfort and kept his eyes on the street as they passed the last buildings of town and headed toward the hills.

"Thomas?" she queried softly. "Is it good for him to work so hard? I know it's none of my business, but he did write about some health problem."

"He's . . . all right," Thomas answered. His discomfort was so obvious he couldn't look at her. "He's fine."

The skepticism gripped her again. If Mike was fine, why was his father so ill at ease with the subject of his son's health that he was squeezing the steering wheel? Yesterday the same subject had shaken Mike.

Judging from their reactions Mike might not be fine, but neither man was willing to discuss it. From her first hour at Aawn she had sensed that Michael and his father were harboring some secret. Was it about Michael's health? Or could it have to do with a creature wandering about in the dark? Or with the past Mike didn't like to talk about? Whatever it was, Katherine was certain the two of them were hiding something important from her.

MIKE WAS AT WORK in the keep tower. His hired workmen were busy around him, and there was conversation going on over the noise of carpenter work and the background music of the popular tapes they played on a small cassette player. Now and again one of the men would shout out his name and repeat some question he had asked, and then Mike would be chided about being "away with the elves," followed by a teasing remark about the woman who had come to the castle yesterday.

The men were right. Mike was so deep in thought about the woman who had come to the castle that he could concentrate on little else for more than a few minutes at a time.

He had never met a woman like her. Her laugh, her smile, the graceful way she moved, her quick mind. Her exquisite beauty. Katherine Glenn was the sort of woman he'd always dreamed about and never met. She was the surprise of his life. There was something about her he could sense and not see . . . something that fascinated him beyond all reason.

While he measured and fitted window frames, Mike's mind was a confusing mixture of joy and sadness. The other females in his life had always been girls playing the roles of women. For a long time he had known about the role-playing, since long before his divorce from Jenny. Other women he had known looked around for a place to fit in—usually the place of most comfort. Katherine was the first woman he had ever met who had created a place for herself, and then occupied it. Everything about her convinced him of this, even though he knew very few facts about her life. He should have read the damn letters as his father had asked him to.

Mike hadn't realized how much his life was lacking, until today. It had been over two years since he divorced Jenny and quit his job and came to Wales to see his eccentric father who had bought, of all the damn things, a genuine Welsh castle. For two years his father had lived here, learning to survive the primitive conditions he seemed to thrive on. Mike came, and fell under the spell of Aawn. Not only had he the ideas to convert the castle into a hotel, but he also had the finances.

Scarcely two years ago Mike had had a house in the Chicago suburbs with two cars in the garage and a seven-to-seven, pressure-filled job and a wife whose life revolved around whose guest list they were on and who accepted or declined her invitations, and the season's latest fashions from Paris. Exactly the life he had sworn he would never have. Exactly the marriage he'd sworn he would never have, with no communication, no meaning and worst of all...no dreams. Jenny's dreams and his could never have found each other.

Now, in the home he could never leave—the haunted castle that had brought Katherine Glenn to Wales—Mike wondered about the dreams of the woman he'd just met. He wondered who she really was. And why he felt as if she had just stepped off the cloud of one of *his* dreams. Every nerve-ending in his body had gone on full alert when Kathy walked into Aawn and into his life. Here was a lady like no other.

And he recognized also that she was disappointed when she met him, although this message was somewhat mixed. She liked his looks ... well, that was a given. His good looks had usually been more of a problem for him than an asset, and it would take more than looks to impress this woman.

Her eyes were mischievous and mysterious. Too deep to read. But he saw himself in her eyes, just the same. He saw the reflection of himself in moments when her thoughts were far away in some secret place she'd never shared with Thomas. Nor shared with anyone.

Yet.

IN MIDAFTERNOON Mike finally came down from the keep tower. Katherine was sitting on a bench in the grassy bailey, petting the dogs, when he emerged from the arched stone entry.

"I finally finished those two window frames," he said. "Dad told me I'd find you here."

She smiled. "I had to plead with him not to feel as if he must play tour guide for me. He finally gave in and let Talbot do the job."

"Dad's legs give out, but he hates to admit he isn't as strong as he once was." Mike lifted the running hose from the nearby garden and began washing sawdust from his hands. "I'm sorry I got so tied up with work. I needed to get some heavy stuff done before the weekend while the guys are here to help."

"Don't be sorry. The last thing I want is to be an inconvenience to you. I've had a super day, Mike. Exploring Aawn is one of the highlights of my life."

"I hope it met your expectations."

"I couldn't have expected what I've found here—the legends come to life. Thomas told me where to find the room where a corpse once disappeared from its casket during a wake and round dragon's stones were found in its place. One can't be in the castle without believing such stories. I begin to imagine streaks of fire breath in the dragon's cave. I hear voices in the corridors."

He gazed at her. "There are voices in the corridors. The voices of the ghosts. But not everyone can hear them."

She stopped breathing. He was serious. "But why... can you and I hear them?"

"Because to us the castle is not dead—it's not a corpse of the past. You and I know it is still alive. And its mysteries and horrors are part of it."

Katherine's heartbeat quickened; she felt the truth of his words. "As fearful as Aawn is, Mike, you love it. Don't you?"

"Yeah. Even more so because it talks to me. It doesn't want to be a dead shell of bygone days. You feel that, too, Kathy, that certain respect for the soul of it, and so the spirits here communicate back."

While he said this, Mike pulled his shirt over his head. He continued the splashing, taking care not to soak the bandage on his upper arm.

Katherine watched in fascination. His arms and chest were heavily muscled, like a swimsuit model's. The water on his tanned skin glistened in sunlight. She felt a fluttering deep inside, and tried to pretend she didn't.

She squared her shoulders in defense of her own weakness. "I see you have an impressive, professional bandage now. Is your arm all right?"

"I have to get myself back to the hospital today for another shot of antibiotics. Hell, I can't sit down from the last one. I had to sleep on my stomach and it gave me a kink in my neck."

"Your father says he doesn't worry as long as you're complaining."

"Then be assured he isn't worried. My complaints come from frustration, I guess. Every time the pain shoots through my arm, the fury in me builds. Not knowing what is creeping around here at night looking for blood is driving me nuts. And this arm is slowing me down when I've got work to do, which makes me even madder."

"Would you have written to me about this—about the attack and about your arm?"

Mike frowned and turned off the hose. "Sure I would have," he answered, but he didn't sound very sure.

"How did you explain your wounds at the hospital?"

"I told them I tripped into broken glass. I doubt the doctor believed it was that simple, but he didn't question it. If you want to ride in with me, I'll be only a few minutes at the doctor and then we could take another route back and I could show you some of the surrounding countryside. We could have a leisure ride and get back in time for dinner."

"It sounds very nice, but shouldn't we help your dad with the cooking?"

"Nah. He cooks every night and enjoys it. Three for dinner is no more work than two. He'll just fry the fish and bake some potatoes and steam some carrots and beans. We have the same meal every night—he just varies the meat and the vegetables. I promised to take you to the less accessible areas of the castle and I will. Either tonight or tomorrow."

"Tomorrow is soon enough. After all these years I can wait one more night."

"Thanks for being patient with me." He dried his arms with his shirt, slid the damp shirt over his head and brushed sawdust from his jeans. "I guess we're headed for town, then."

IN THE TRUCK, while he drove, she asked, "Are you aware of how the townspeople gossip about you?"

"I am. But you just got here. How could you know about the gossip?"

"How could I not? Even the clerk at the stationer's shop, Cadi Morgan, knew you brought me into town yesterday."

"I suppose small towns everywhere are the same."

"I'm sure they are. And a person from another culture is sure to be noticed, especially when that person is a handsome, eligible bachelor."

With eyes fixed on the gravel road, he said mildly, "At least the bachelor part is irrefutable."

"And the handsome part."

Mike smiled mischievously. "The eligible part is where they're wrong, then."

"Really? Why are you not eligible? Surely not because you're too busy refurbishing a castle."

"Isn't that a good reason?"

His tone was teasing. Katherine's leveled into a monotone. "Castles live a thousand years. They're legacies left by kings and lords, and by ordinary men who fight to save them from the ravages of time. Castles stand on and on as if forever. Men do not."

He cleared his throat. "My obsession over this project is only part of the reason I'm not looking for a wife. The real reason is that I've tried it. I was married. It ended. I have no desire to go through something like that again."

His sudden candor was raw and unexpected. She said, "You wrote very little about your wife. I knew her loss was painful for you to talk about. I could tell you deeply loved her."

Mike winced and drew a quick breath. His fist tightened on the steering wheel.

The subject of his deceased wife was too devastating for him to deal with, she thought. The years hadn't healed his grief. Even now, the pain was written all over his face.

"Kathy, look, I . . . I can't . . ." He pounded the steering wheel in a burst of anger. "Damn it, I can't continue this—"

She reached out swiftly to touch his arm. "It's all right! It's normal to feel anger and resentment toward a loved one who has died and left us. It's part of the grieving process."

He muttered an inaudible oath.

"Please," he said, half-choking. "I'm not—"

Patting his arm, she interrupted. "I understand. We won't talk about your wife anymore."

The hills sloped steadily toward the village. Katherine set her eyes on the green landscape and they rode in silence for a time. His discomfort was so strong she could feel it like electric vibrations.

After a time she turned back to study his face. "Your eyes look angry one minute, Mike, and then the next minute they look so sad."

"I'm not sad."

"What are you thinking about?"

"Spiders."

"Good heavens!"

"Did you ever watch a spider spin a web?"

"Yes. It's both fascinating and horrifying. Such intricate designs, as though they understood design. I've often wondered if spiders realize how beautiful their death snares are."

"I doubt it. I think they just stupidly spin them. Stupidly and cruelly. They have no brains."

Something had gone wrong with this conversation. Mike was talking in riddles, and she hated that. "What the devil are you talking about?"

His brow was creased in a frown. "Are you afraid of spiders?"

Katherine tensed. "I hate to admit it, but yes, I'm terrified of them. Are there spiders in the dark corners of your castle?"

"I'm afraid so," he answered softly. "Not cunning ones. Stupid ones."

5

SHE WAITED in the reception room of what she thought must be the smallest hospital in the world. Thoughts about Mike assailed and depressed her. On the surface, other men would envy him. His money. His good looks. But fate took away as well as gave. He had loved and lost. In his short life he had been dealt his share of pain.

She would not ask what his wife died of; one didn't ask that question. But, thinking about it, Katherine was beginning to understand why Mike had taken long, quiet evenings to write contemplative letters to her when other men his age would be tearing around with the adoring girls of the village—believing as all youths that life lasts forever. Mike knew better. This was what he meant when he told her he was older than he looked. Gradually the old Michael, her friend, was showing through. But only a little.

The hospital building was two hundred years old and looked it. Built originally as a private dwelling, it had long, narrow windows and high ceilings. The many layers of paint on the walls were cracked and chipped in the corners and around the window frames. Two landscape prints with grazing horses hung on the wall. A receptionist's desk was placed in an alcove in the hallway down which Mike had disappeared when summoned to an examining room. Every few minutes Katherine would catch the receptionist glancing up at her curiously. *Now I suppose it will be all over town that I sat here waiting for Mike to see a doctor*, she thought. In fifteen minutes he returned, pulling at the fresh bandage under his shirt.

Once outside she asked, "Is your arm all right?"

"Yeah. Getting better. You were right about it, Kathy. I'd have been in trouble if I hadn't listened to you and come in yesterday. You must be good for me. When I first laid eyes on you, I said to myself, 'This lady is good for me.'"

"Of course you did."

He smiled and opened the passenger door of the truck. "Do you want to know what I really thought?"

"I'm not sure."

He closed the door, walked around to the driver's side and settled behind the wheel. "I thought you were beautiful."

"I'm not beautiful."

"If you don't think so, your eyesight is impaired. I, on the other hand, have perfect eyesight."

Your eyesight, along with everything else, she thought. He had flirted in his letters, too. Katherine had become accustomed to his very civilized flirtations. But it was a far greater matter now, from a man who so reeked of masculine sexuality that the least provocation roused her senses to full alert. Katherine wondered if he was aware of his effect on women. Of course he was, and if asked he'd probably admit it.

She felt oddly helpless. It was not a familiar sensation and it made her resentful, both of him and of her own reactions to him. She was a mature woman tingling like a silly schoolgirl.

Sitting beside him, her legs touching his now and then when the rough road bounced them, she was so aware of the physical contact it was hard to concentrate on his comments about the scenery. What kind of con was she pulling on herself with this "mature woman" stuff? The spinster of Allendale was a tag others gave her. Why the hell was she trying to tell herself she wore it in Mike Reese's eyes? She had hidden behind the false perception of others to guard the wildness of her secret self. But she didn't have to hide behind it here. . . .

Here she was not the spinster of Allendale. She was Kathy. She was free! The winter's cocoon was shed and gone.

Mike drove for an hour through the Welsh countryside, over crooked, narrow roads, past farmhouses, through villages. He pointed out landmarks, pronouncing the Welsh names with ease.

They parked at the side of a road and walked out on a bridge to watch a pair of swans swimming in the calm, reed-poked shore waters of the low river beneath them. "And me without my camera," she lamented, resting her elbows on the rail of the old stone bridge.

"The swans are always here. We'll have a picnic sometime, over on the shore. I can picture us right over there on a sunny afternoon, eating fresh-baked bread and drinking wine."

Katherine pictured it, too. The grass looked soft and velvety under the trees and wildflowers were blooming everywhere. She said, "There must be other excellent picnic spots along the lakeshore at Aawn."

"Yeah, there are. We even have swans visit us now and then. And ducks. This place, though, has always drawn me. It's the peace of it, I guess—the sound of the river gurgling by. This river is never in a hurry."

"You like peace more than anything, don't you?"

He gazed at her with a look Katherine couldn't interpret, except that it was coming from deep inside him, from his heart.

"Yeah, I like peace. My stint of being embroiled in corporate America made me a lot of money, but the turmoil was driving me out of my mind. I'd be wearing a plastic wristband with a number on it if I hadn't gotten out. I pity all those others who are still there, chained to the madness." He smiled wistfully. "My friends back in Chicago, whom I'm rarely in contact with anymore, accuse me of being a hopeless chaser of dreams, an escapist. Pitiful, isn't it? Just look at the beauty of this place. Just feel the silence. Nothing would ever induce me to go back."

"You left the carnival for the real world."

"Yes, I did, Kathy. Do you realize how few people can see it like that?"

"Probably not. I live so far out of that frantic world myself, I can do no more than imagine. I've often wondered how sensitive people stand it."

"Some of us can't. There's this uncontrollable pull toward...toward..." He hesitated.

"Toward nature," she finished.

He closed his eyes. "Exactly. You know about that pull!"

"Yes, I do know."

He smiled. "I guessed your feelings about nature. There are so many things I feel I know about you."

He made the strangest remarks, Katherine thought, for a man who had been reading her letters for years.

"Of course you know a lot about me," she said softly.

He didn't take his eyes from the gently flowing water beneath them. "You mean the letters."

She frowned. "Sometimes I detect almost a bitterness at the mention of the letters. As well as a very poor memory on your part about the things we've discussed."

His shoulders heaved in a sigh. "I want to think of us as having just met. Admittedly, we are both different from what the other expected, and I want to get to know you now...as if we had no past. Does that make sense?"

"I suppose it does. I've asked myself why you're so different in life than in letters. It's rather baffling. Did you mislead me deliberately?"

"No," he said. "Did you mislead...me...deliberately?"

She straightened. "What do you mean?"

Mike shrugged. His shoulder touched hers again as they leaned on the railing of the bridge. "I just had this picture of you as kind of drab and...older." He smiled. "Like you thought of me. Aren't we a pair of rare birds, camouflaging the colors of our feathers? Let's just...go from here. Okay?"

She nodded. What he said made a certain sense. Confused as she was about her man of letters, Mike had a legitimate reason to ask if she herself had done some misleading. She had, and now he knew it. And he had, and she knew it. And what was the point in belaboring all that now?

Mike said, "We were talking about getting close to the peace of nature. To me it's the best part of living. I'm never going to make a fabulous living with my castle inn, but it'll be enough to live on, if I ever get it opened. It's a hell of a difficult project I've taken on, but I love it. How many guys own a castle? I'm the luckiest guy I know."

Katherine smiled dreamily and watched the two swans glide together and touch their long, graceful necks to each other. A gesture of gentle love. The river sang a soft and haunting song as it moved below them. In the descending twilight, each reed cast a slender, slanted shadow over the water. A thrush warbled overhead.

Mike moved his hand over hers on the railing, and stood in silence. Was it her imagination, or was his hand slightly trembling when he touched her?

It was not her imagination. He pressed his fingers against hers with a sensual, intimate movement that caused her heartbeat to quicken because his touch was that of a lover, not a friend. It wasn't possible he could think of her like that! Not this . . . this Mike! Nor was it possible for her to think of him . . . like that . . . this handsome young hunk in his early twenties.

Not possible!

Then why was his hand trembling over hers? And why was her heart trembling out of control? Katherine held her breath for fear its rapid pace would give her away.

His gaze remained on the trees along the riverbank, where he was looking for the singing thrush. "Kathy, I'm glad you came."

"You say that as if you hadn't expected to be glad."

"I'm more glad than I thought I'd be."

"So am I."

"You are?" His hand continued to caress hers. "You weren't successful at hiding your shock when you first saw me."

"Neither were you, as a matter of fact."

"Yeah." His voice was husky. "Well. Here we are now."

"Yes." She felt the warm caresses of his hand on hers and the nearness of his body next to her, and the confusion that pulsed in her bloodstream. "Yes. Here we are now."

DINNER WAS A CORDIAL AFFAIR—a meal in a castle tower where lords and ladies of past centuries dined on the identical fare of fresh lake salmon and vegetables grown in the bailey garden. Afterward, over coffee and Irish cream liqueur, Thomas smoked his pipe and recited poetry.

Katherine said, "You come by your love of poetry honestly, Mike."

"Yeah," Mike answered, relaxing on the sofa near the fire.

"Can you recite it, too?"

"Nah, not a bit."

"Sure you can. You often quoted poetry in your letters."

"You've caught me. I'm a fake."

"Don't listen to him, Katherine," Thomas said. "Mike appreciates poetry a great deal. He just doesn't want me to know he admitted it to you in his letters. In fact, we sit around here on long nights talking about poetry and literature. He favors Walt Whitman."

"*Leaves of Grass?* I love *Leaves of Grass.* In our letters you barely mentioned Walt Whitman, Mike."

Mike shot his father a quick, sharp glance. "Dad lies."

Thomas laughed. "We have no secrets here. Mike can wallow in Whitman as happily as a pig in mud. Come on, lad, give us a few lines. Do it for Katherine."

"I'm not in the mood."

"You always were before—in the letters," she coaxed.

"There, you see," Thomas said. "Do you want this poor girl to think you misrepresented yourself?"

Mike glared at his father with a vengeance Katherine couldn't comprehend. He was still glaring at him as he reached for the book on the end table. He began to read in a deep, throaty voice, slowly, intensely, almost vengefully.

"It is I, you women, I make my way,
I am stern, acrid, large, undissuadable, but I love you,
I do not hurt you any more than is necessary for you,
I pour the stuff to start sons and daughters fit for these States, I press with slow rude muscle,
I brace myself effectually, I listen to no entreaties,
I dare not withdraw till I deposit what had so long accumulated within me.

Through you I drain the pent-up rivers of myself,
In you I wrap a thousand onward years . . ."

He stopped only with hesitancy and the silence filled in around him.

Katherine sat stunned. The suggestive sensuality of his voice had brought forth pictures of the poet's vivid phrases and made her tremble. Mike's face and his body were fixed indelibly upon her memory with those erotic images. She feared he knew very well the effect of the poet's words.

Thomas glared. "A crude stunt."

"You asked for Walt. Walt you got." He turned. "Kathy, should I apologize?"

"No." She straightened, outwardly showing complete control. "I find the passage remarkable."

He grinned. "There, Dad! Kathy appreciates the words of the world's greatest poet, too."

"I admit to a deep love for Whitman's work," Katherine said, wondering why Mike's attitude toward his father seemed so defiant. The passage in question was a few short lines buried among many thousands. Mike knew the book well in order to find that page so quickly. Why he was acting defensive about the poetry was puzzling.

Thomas obviously considered the stunt appalling. He puffed at his pipe, squinting at his son with an expression she couldn't identify. Something was strained between them.

"Katherine," Thomas said suddenly, as if to change the subject, "have you ever fished?"

"Not since I was a child and my father used to take me."

"I fish every morning when the weather permits. Why don't you join me? Mike won't ever tear himself away from work."

"If I did, it wouldn't be to fish," Mike said. "Fishing bores me silly. However, later tomorrow I will tear myself away to give Kathy a tour of the dungeons of Aawn." He propped his feet on a wood chest that served as a table in front of the sofa. "I'll take you to the dragon's cave under the castle. Did you know it's a natural cave?"

"Surely you told her so in your letters," Thomas said.

"Did I?" he asked her.

She squinted at him. "Why do you pretend not to remember? We discussed at length—and both concurred—that the cave originally inspired the dragon legend."

He shrugged. "When I first heard about the cave, I assumed it was man-made, an escape tunnel in case of siege. But it isn't. It's a natural cave with an entrance from the lowest passage of the gatehouse. The ancients must have used it for storage or maybe for a dungeon, although they built another formidable dungeon near it. I'll show you tomorrow, if you're not afraid to enter the lair of the beast."

"It's the place where you were attacked?"

"Close. I was in the passage leading to the cave. And I have some serious misgivings about taking you down there."

"It's what I came all this way to see!"

"I know. I know. I promised to take you. Are you going to try the fishing in the morning?"

"Sure. It might be fun."

"We've a date, then," Thomas said. "I'll call for you early at Mrs. Mills's."

"It isn't necessary. I've decided to rent a bicycle."

"Good lord, you can't cycle out. It's uphill."

"Downhill going back. I'll enjoy it."

"It's a shocking idea, Katherine. The ride would be grueling."

She laughed. "I'm used to grueling exercise. It keeps me healthy. What time do you start?"

"The fishing is good from eight until midmorning."

"Fine. I'll be here."

DURING THE DRIVE to the village, Mike's attention tended to wander from their conversation; something else was on his mind. He had become curious about Katherine's private life—the one she didn't write to his father about, the one she didn't talk to him about. A woman as attractive as she would have men in love with her, or worse, one certain man. Yet from the way his father had talked, the roots of a romance had sprouted in their correspondence. Something about Thomas had attracted her—his love of poetry, his sophistication, his appreciation of the small and beautiful things in life, and his sense of adventure. Thomas had, after all, been the one to discover the Castle of Aawn. Hell, Mike thought, he himself had all the same qualities. Maybe not the intense love for poetry but he might develop it by the time he reached his father's age.

His father's age. Katherine had not realized her man of letters, as Thomas said she called him, was in his sixties. What had Kathy really come looking for—a dragon or a man? A surge of jealousy assaulted Mike— jealousy of every man who knew Kathy or ever had. Jealousy of his father because it was his father she learned to like so much and his father she had come to see. She would justifiably be furious if she knew Mike was an imposter.

But she was going to have to know. This stupid lie was going to have to be resolved, and soon.

They reached the bed-and-breakfast. He waited while Katherine checked with Mrs. Mills about the bicycle. A five-speed bike was parked on the back porch, polished and waiting.

In the foyer of the boarding house, Mike squeezed her hand to say good-night. He hesitated and held on, looking hard into her eyes, trying to read her thoughts.

She met his gaze, watching his eyes darken, and worrying that he could hear her heart start to pound. She scolded herself for the pounding. What was it about this man? First he intrigued her with his words on paper, and now he was doing it with his eyes and his touch...but it was nothing like it was supposed to be. Everything was so wrong...so ridiculously wrong....

"I'll see you tomorrow," he muttered, and then smiled with mischief. "And don't worry about tomorrow, Kathy. About the dragon's cave, I mean. You'll be down there with me."

THOMAS WAS STILL UP, reading by the fire, when Mike returned. "I suppose you're reading poetry," Mike said sarcastically as he threw his coat over a hook.

"I think we've had quite enough poetry for one night, thanks to you."

"I couldn't take your goading, and your lies to Kathy."

"So you took it out on her by reading something erotic."

"Maybe I shouldn't have," Mike conceded. "But it turns out Kathy isn't the prude you had us both convinced she is."

"You're quite right about that. She's far more vibrant than I'd imagined."

Mike began rummaging through desk drawers. "Where are her letters? I want to read them."

Thomas raised his eyebrows. "Oh? After I pleaded with you to read them before she came and you would have none of it?"

"I keep tripping up. I don't know what you've told her." Mike lifted out a neat stack of letters from the drawer and brought them to the sofa. The dogs were curled contentedly on their rugs. The castle had fallen into its deathlike night silence. "Do you realize she thinks my wife died? And worse than that, she thinks I spent last winter being sick."

"Of course she would think so." Thomas puffed on his pipe. "It's what I wrote to her." Cursing, Mike took out one of the letters and began to read. The letter was newsy, not personal. She wrote about an art exhibit and about the first spring blossoms on the lilac trees. He pictured her standing by the lilacs in a summer dress, the breeze blowing through her hair. He saw her reach out to pick a flower, and deeply breathe in its fragrance as she held the lilacs against her cheek.

Swallowing, he looked up. "Dad, this charade has gone on long enough. It's ridiculous and it's mean. I'm going to tell her the truth. She'll hate us both and rightly so, but I have to tell her."

His father shot to his feet. "You can't!"

"It won't be easy. But it will be easier than carrying on with this stupid lie."

Panic contorted Thomas's face. "Mike, you wouldn't betray me like that. You, my own flesh and blood. I can't believe you could do that to me."

He tossed down the letter. "What about *her*, Dad?"

"Katherine has only a short time here. Then she'll go back to her life, taking the memories with her. And it will be over. Try to think how embarrassed she'll be if you tell her now. And as for me—the humiliation would kill me." His eyes fixed pleadingly on those of his son. "The humiliation would *kill* me, Mike. I couldn't face her. The situation would be intolerable. *Please.* Have some compassion for this wretched old man. Don't do that to me."

Mike swore a violent oath. "How the hell did you talk me into this mess in the first place? You and your false pride."

"False pride?" Thomas blinked repeatedly. "Is that what you think it is?"

"Yes. And it's got all three of us into an intolerable situation." He pounded a fist into his palm. "I just can't live with it, even for a month."

"Well, you're going to. For all our sakes. She'll feel like a fool, too, you know. She might be angry enough to leave. Or is that what this is about? You want her to leave?"

"No, as a matter of fact, I don't."

His father puffed at his pipe. "I didn't think so. I've seen how you look at her. I'm sure she's seen it, too. This hermit existence hasn't been good for you, my boy."

Anger was building in Mike. He seldom became really angry with his father, but it was happening now. Thomas was a skilled manipulator, and even though his son was aware of it, too often he was unable to resist. Thomas was impossible to reason with when it served his interests to be unreasonable. And Mike understood the humiliation Thomas would suffer if Katherine discovered he couldn't face her as an old man. Mike had never known anyone who fought aging like his father did.

"I'm a dying man," Thomas said.

Mike rose and began to pace. "Now you're blackmailing me with threats that your heart couldn't take the blow if Katherine finds out we lied to her?"

"Maybe it couldn't. It would be the worst indignity of my life."

"Great. And this from the father who taught me the value of truth. Dad, I can't stand lying to her."

"She'll be gone soon and I'll still be here—or what hollow shell is left of me after you destroy me. After you strip away every shred of my dignity...and a good part of her dignity with it."

"Oh, please! Stop it."

Thomas Reese stood over his son, looking older to Mike than he had ever seen him. His hair was almost completely white. His beard was white. His shoulders were stooped. His deeply veined fists were clenched.

"Listen to me," he pleaded in a voice Mike had never heard before. "You don't understand. For me this thing with Katherine has been hard, very hard. Do you know that your mother was the only woman I ever loved? The only woman I ever dated? We married when we were only kids, and there were only the two of us for fourteen years. It was fourteen years before you were born! In all those years, your mother was my life and I was hers. I have never been any good without her. No good at all. Katherine's letters took away some of my loneliness, filled some of my need. Grant me my insecurity, Mike. You don't have to like it, but I'm pleading with you to tolerate it. Let me have my pride. Please."

Mike had always known of his father's devotion to his mother. Since her death Thomas had had no thoughts of seeing other women. He had isolated himself in a castle tower, and the only woman in his life had been Katherine. Thomas didn't want reality any longer. This was what his plea was all about.

Hurting for his dad, Mike answered, "I'll never forgive you for putting Kathy and me through this."

Thomas reached down and squeezed his son's shoulder, a gesture of affection he had used since Mike was a small boy. "Forgiveness I don't need, nor ask for, my lad. I ask only for understanding, which you've given me. Now, how about a nip of brandy before we go to bed?"

"No, thanks. I don't feel like drinking. I feel like hell over this mess. I'm just going to look over these letters."

His father smiled as he poured himself a drink with shaking hands. "Ah, yes, Katherine's letters. I understand perfectly. If I were a young man who had just met Miss Katherine Glenn, I'd be wanting to know her better, too."

To this, Michael had no counter. He retreated into his anger and began to read.

"We're not as different as you like to think we are," Thomas said while he made his rounds, straightening the room.

Presently Pembroke raised her head and sniffed. Talbot, too, was roused from his sleep. Mike looked up from the letter he was reading. "Sulphur," he said.

He rose and put on a jacket. "Why are we smelling sulphur all the way up here? I'm going to investigate."

"Maybe you shouldn't," his father said. "After what happened the last time."

Mike buttoned the jacket and took his hunting knife from a shelf. "I'll stay out of the dungeon areas," he lied. "I'll just look around the keep. It's one thing to smell that sulphur in the dragon's gatehouse tower but, damn it, the keep is where we live. I'm not going to let some smelly phantom, human or otherwise, scare me out of my home."

Thomas frowned. "Still, you need to be careful."

Checking the flashlight, Mike answered, "It's a prankster. There's never been anything in the keep except the smell and a few sounds from the ghosts. Ghosts are harmless enough." From the doorway, with Talbot at his side, he turned. "I'll find nothing and probably end up working off some of my frustration by sanding some counters in the hall. My usual fun-filled evening."

He ducked into the stairwell. The sulphur smell seldom reached the keep tower; it was the massive gatehouse, with its high, empty tower rooms and curving passages and its horrible dungeon and its cave, where the signs of the dragon were usually found. As Mike descended the dark, spiraling stairs, the faint odor became stronger. It was coming from the lower levels of the gatehouse. Since the attack, he had been certain a human intruder was slinking around playing dragon, and each day since, his anger had intensified.

He stepped out into the bailey and the crisp night air. The sky was spangled with stars and a three-quarter moon hung low in the sky, casting an eerie glow behind the silhouettes of the towers that surrounded him. The castle absorbed darkness like a night predator; it drank darkness thirstily and settled back in profound silence, shutting out the modern century that rendered it useless, merely a curiosity and a memory. In the silence of night, the castle remembered more noisy times, and its ghost remembered, and Mike remembered. It was at night, in the silence, that the castle came alive again.

Determined to find out its secrets, and armed only with a knife, Mike and the dog moved into the black shadow of the dragon's tower.

6

KATHERINE'S FASCINATION for castles and dragons began in childhood with the fairy stories her mother read to her. On trips to the children's library, she brought home books about fairy kings and queens, and read them over and over. There were princes in those kingdoms, and knights in shining armor who slew firebreathing dragons. In her girlhood daydreams, Katherine was a princess, and her knight in shining armor wore a red lion on his breastplate and carried his lady's lace handkerchief next to his heart.

At university she learned the strengths of legends and their importance in the cultural makeup of people. She studied superstition and its influence on ancient and modern societies, and came to realize that in most of the world it was impossible to draw a line between history and myth because one merged into the other. In her graduate thesis Katherine had determined that there was a time in British history when a belief in living dragons was accepted.

Her father often ridiculed the "flighty, impractical" side of her and accused her of being a hopeless dreamer. Katherine acknowledged that she did, indeed, sometimes live in a world of fantasy, and she found nothing wrong with that. To avoid ridicule, though, she had kept her dreams to herself. And when her summers became summers of impractical daydreams—the travelling circus—those, too, she kept to herself. Allendale was too small and smug to accept unconventional behavior from one of its respected educators.

This morning, bicycling from Llanhafod to the medieval Castle of Aawn, Katherine remembered her daydreams in vivid, living colors. The reds and yellows of tournament flags, the sun sparkling on silver armor. The castle gates flung open to welcome a mysterious knight on a blue-black horse draped with the silk banner of the red lion. Her knight. Her castle. The memories made her smile.

How her daydreams had tottered and shifted was unsettling, at best. This Welsh summer, she had come to find a scholarly gentleman and found instead a reckless knight. In childhood she had wanted the knight. She was a woman now, with a woman's less whimsical daydreams.

Damn, though. The mystical dreams had never really left. Being at Aawn with Michael made her understand that what was reality for her was fantasy for other people. The Katherine of Allendale was the fraud. The person she was now in the summer of dreams—the self she knew best—belonged here.

In the shadow of Aawn, Katherine couldn't see Thomas on the lakeshore. She parked her bicycle by the castle gate and looked for him amid the ferns and birches at the water's edge, but was greeted only by the birds, and two squirrels scampering through the long grass. Her legs were tired, even though the last quarter mile of her journey, along the tree-lined lane, was almost level.

Thomas was not at the lake at all, but in the courtyard, talking to a workman. Both dogs were frolicking on the grass; the two men were paying no attention to them. When Thomas saw her approach he broke away from the conversation and walked across the lawn to meet her. As he came closer, she saw deep worry lines on his face.

"What is it, Thomas? Is something wrong?"

"Very possibly, Katherine. Mike didn't show up for breakfast and his bed hasn't been slept in. Both the truck and car are here, so he must be somewhere in the castle."

Katherine's heartbeat quickened. She clearly remembered the claw marks on his arm.

"His bed wasn't slept in? Can you be sure?"

"Mike has never made a bed in his life. I do it, and his bed is just as I made it up yesterday morning."

Fear gripped her. "Oh, Thomas. Where would he be? Did you see him after he got back from the village last night?"

"Yes. We talked for a while. Then we smelled the sulphur. Mike took a knife and he and Talbot went to investigate. "I didn't hear them come back. The dog, as you can see, is fine, but I'm getting extremely worried."

"Have you asked the workmen to look for him?"

"Not yet. I've been putting it off as long as I dared, thinking Mike would show up at any minute. If I alert the men, there will be new rumors, and nothing would upset Mike more. However, I think I'm out of options. We're going to have to begin a search. I don't dare join in myself. Nobody needs a collapsing old man to add to the problem."

"I can look," she said. "I can take the dogs."

"Not on your life, Katherine. There is danger in the castle. We'll have to get the—"

He halted abruptly, his attention riveted on the entrance of the gatehouse. Katherine turned.

Mike was ducking through the gateway. There was a smudge of dirt on his forehead, and the expression on his face was strangely blank. He seemed dazed.

Overcome with relief, they hurried toward him.

"Mike!" Thomas said. "Where the devil have you been?"

"Why? What time is it?"

"Nearly nine-thirty, for God's sake. I was worried sick when you didn't show up for breakfast."

Mike was rubbing his forehead as if it ached. "Time got away from me."

Katherine and Thomas exchanged glances. Thomas touched his son's shoulder. "You don't sound normal or look normal. What in hell is wrong with you? What has happened?"

"I've just been poking around the castle," he answered in a thin, brittle voice.

"And? Did you find anything?"

Mike looked away. "I was set for another encounter with a claw, but it didn't come. There was nothing...human down there." He cleared his throat. "Sorry for my bad manners, Kathy. I haven't said good morning. Why aren't you fishing?"

"We were about to issue an all-points bulletin."

"For what?"

She glanced at his father, then back to him. "After the attack last week, and now being missing for hours, you can ask?"

Mike rubbed his neck, moving his head stiffly in a circular motion. "I wish the damn thing would attack again. This time I'll be ready."

Thomas shifted from one leg to another in frustration. "Is your brain disengaged? You look like you've crawled through a war zone. Are you trying to tell us you spent the entire night just wandering around the castle?"

"Yeah," Mike answered thinly. "Did you leave some breakfast for me? I'm starving." He looked from one to the other. "Hey, why the long faces? Why don't you two go on down to the lake and catch dinner? I'll get some food and a shower and go to work."

His words were controlled, but the expression in his eyes was not. Mike looked at Katherine with such confusion that it filled her with fear. Almost horror. Something *had* happened in the castle last night. Mike looked like hell and he was badly shaken. His clothes were so covered with dust he looked as if he had been rolling in it.

Still rubbing his neck, he walked to the keep while they stood on the grass, looking at each other, bewildered.

"This behavior isn't like him," Thomas said.

"He looks exhausted."

"And traumatized. Damned weird, this. There's not much we can do but wait until he decides to talk about it."

She said, "He was somewhere in the castle all night and lost track of time? How is that possible?"

"Let's give him some time to get himself together. Then we'll start grilling him. In the meantime, we might as well be fishing as pacing."

WHEN THEY CAME IN from the lake two hours later, Katherine was feeling the tensed nerves knotting in her shoulders. Thomas suggested she help herself to a juice and a pastry upstairs while he went about the chore of cleaning their catch. The fish hadn't noticed their restlessness; the fishermen had done well.

On the way up she stopped off at the Great Hall, where sounds of the workmen's saws and hammers echoed off the stone walls. From the doorway she scanned the room, but Mike was not there.

She found him one level above, in the living quarters, sitting on the sofa with his head buried in his hands. On the table in front of him was a glass of water. He sat as still as death, except for the movement of his broad shoulders as he breathed. The fear she had felt in the courtyard came sweeping back.

Katherine approached cautiously. "Mike?"

When he raised his head, his hair fell across his eyes.

"Mike, are you all right?"

"I'm too tired to work."

"I'm not surprised, after being up all night. You look like a zombie. You're even acting like a zombie."

He swept the hair away from his eyes and drank down the glass of water.

She asked, "Do you want some more?"

He nodded. She picked up the glass, filled it from the bottled water in the kitchen and brought it back to him.

"Thanks."

She watched him drink.

"Where's Dad?" he asked. "Cleaning fish?"

"Yes."

Mike set down the glass. "Then if we're alone, I'd better tell you, Kathy. I saw a dragon last night. There is a dragon in the cave."

She lowered herself onto the sofa beside him, her heart beating so fast she had to gulp in air to try to calm herself.

"A small one," Mike said. "And dead. But it's a dragon, there's no question of that."

Katherine slid back against the cushions, with all the feeling drained from her limbs.

Mike's voice came flat and weak. "In the cave there's an area I'd never explored before last night. I came upon a well-preserved skeleton in that chamber of the cave. A fossilized dragon is down there."

She drew in her breath. "That's impossible!"

"It's there—the strangest-looking thing I've ever seen."

"But no actual dragon has ever lived! They're imaginary!"

"This one isn't."

She felt like shaking him back to reason. "But it . . . can't be! It has to be some . . . animal."

"With wings?"

"Oh, no. Wings?"

"The skull and legs are reptilian. After two college biology labs, I'm not completely ignorant on the subject."

She was unaware that her fingernails were digging into his arm. "How big is it?"

"Eight or nine feet long. Wingspan a couple of feet at the widest point. You're about to draw blood on my arm, Kathy."

She stared at him. "What you're saying is not possible. You do realize that, don't you?"

"Of course I realize it. I realize no living reptile looks anything like this thing. My arm?"

She released her grip reluctantly.

He said, "These bones aren't old enough for the Cretaceous age—it can't be a seventy-five-million-year-old dinosaur—that I know for sure. Do you have any idea what this means, if that thing is real?"

She stammered, "It can't be . . . true . . . it simply can't."

"I repeat. Do you know what it means, if it is?"

The words would barely come. "It means dragons are real."

"And the legend is real, too."

"You're saying the beast actually lived and recently enough to be contemporary with humans in this castle? Oh, Mike, come on! That's utterly ridiculous and you know it!"

"I do know it. I also know what's down there. I spent the whole night crawling around the cave on my hands and knees, searching that cave floor... for a human artifact, another bone, anything. But I didn't find anything else. I think I was too dazed to think rationally."

When Katherine tried to take a deep breath, her breath caught in her throat and she nearly choked. "It's terrifying to try to imagine the implications of this."

"Or what will happen if this information gets out."

"You can't keep it secret!"

He touched her hand. "I don't know *what* the hell to do about it. I know we have to find out what the thing is, but I don't want to turn this place into a circus. You've studied dragons. What do you know about dragon bones?"

"There aren't any. As for the myths, they come from several places in the world, but from Britain more than anywhere else. The dragons of the Far East were very different from Western dragons—different looks, different temperament. Some scholars think the concept of dragons came to Rome from China in early days of trade and then spread from Rome upward to northern Europe. Others believe the myths originated from actual animals that were seen or imagined, and stories built on rumor and exaggeration. I'm of the second school of thought. I've always believed the British concepts originated in Britain, even though we know there was some Roman influence. The stories go back as far as the earliest written languages here. Remember Beowulf?"

"The early stories were written by people who could not possibly have known about dinosaurs."

"Definitely not. You have to show me this dragon!"

"Preferably before we hit Dad with the story so you can verify what I'm saying and he can't plot to have me committed. Actually, I don't want to put any more stress on him than necessary. He has a heart condition. So I think you should see this skeleton first and tell me it's a dead cow."

Katherine rose. "Come on, then. Show me this cow that died in a cave with a big-winged bird stuck on its back."

He began replacing the batteries of two oversize flashlights. Katherine, watching him, asked, "Surely you weren't crawling around on your hands and knees for the whole night?"

"I sat and stared into blackness much of the time. I turned off my light and just sat in total darkness, total silence. And no sense of time. I let the cave swallow me and tried to imagine what living thing would ever wander down there. When I came out, I had no idea whether it was night or day. Okay, we've got fresh batteries. Let's go."

They met Thomas crossing the inner ward. He was carrying a pan of cleaned fish, which Mike took time to admire. "I promised to take Kathy on the perilous tour," he told his father. "Afterward we'll be up for some lunch."

Thomas scowled. "How long do you plan to keep me in suspense over what you saw last night?"

"I found some animal bones in the cave. Old bones, probably fossils. I spent the night searching for more. When we get back, I'll give you the details."

His father's eyes rolled skyward. "Katherine, how can you stand it?"

They did not cross the bailey to reach the gatehouse. Instead, Mike led her there through an inner passage of the castle, a walkway from which several rooms opened—small chambers once used for storing weapons.

When they reached an interior entry into the dragon's tower, Mike said, "The gatehouse and keep foundations date back to the twelfth century. I wonder if invading enemies actually believed the castle was guarded by a dragon."

The tower stairway was shrouded in darkness. Wind blowing through the high window slits sounded like the shrieks of ghosts. Yesterday Katherine had climbed up to the far reaches of the empty tower and felt the presence of the ghosts while standing at the top gazing out over the lake and the peaceful countryside dotted with grazing sheep. But, as Mike had requested, she hadn't ventured into the depths below. Now he led her there. She followed, not uttering a sound to disturb the echoes, and she was glad for the security of the grip of his hand.

At the bottom he said, "Dungeon level."

They were standing before a pitch-dark passage, stone above them and stone below. The silence as deep as eternity. What was it like, Katherine wondered with a shiver, to be led in chains to this cold stone dungeon . . . to glimpse it in the narrow light of fire torches held by captors, knowing the fire torches would soon retreat and blackness would fall like a cape of death.

Such a fate had befallen many a poor soul. The ghosts of the dungeon had known death before dying; she could imagine their wails of anguish echoing in the darkness.

Halfway down the black passage Mike stopped and flashed his light on the stone floor. "Bloodstains. This is where I was attacked. And over here . . ." He moved the light. "These drops of blood aren't mine. I wasn't over here at all. Talbot either bit or badly scratched the attacker."

The loudness of his voice frightened Katherine. *Shh, they'll hear us,* she wanted to warn, having no clear idea of who *they* were. She tried, instead, to lighten the cloud of foreboding. "Maybe Talbot killed the thing and it went off to die and you have found its bones."

He squeezed her hand. "A woman who can joke even when she's shaking with fear is my kind of woman."

"I'm not afraid, not of some dried bones. I'm shaking with excitement."

"The dungeon pit is just over there," he said, shining his light into the darkness. She followed the beam toward a black hole with a few iron bars over the top.

"Hang on to me. Don't fall."

"Such a deep pit! We must be very far under the ground."

Mike said, "The pit is the dungeon proper. Can you imagine being thrown down there never to be seen alive again? A rope ladder was lowered and raised, when needed, but I doubt even a rat could scale these walls. Food was thrown down to the wretched captives, but they couldn't have lived long in the damp and cold. I brought in a rope ladder and went down once to look at the scratches and some drawings scraped on the walls by the prisoners."

"Mike, it's hideous!"

"The fact that they didn't use the cave itself as a dungeon has always made me think there might be a passage out of the castle through the cave. But if there is a way out, no one has found it."

The cave entrance was some twelve meters from the pit. They had to double over to get through the low, narrow opening, but inside, the ceiling was ten or twelve feet high. Katherine shone her light around the stone formations. "A dry cave!"

"Dry enough for preserving bones. You are now in the heart of the dragon's lair." He took a sharp turn right, crawled over some formations into another cavern, and still another, while she followed, her heart thundering.

Finally he stopped and shone his light on the cavern floor. Katherine gasped. The skeleton lay before her— body, head, wings. The thin bones of one wing were spread in a pattern, the bones of the other wing were heaped together.

"I can't believe this!" she whispered.

"The wing bones are hollow, like a bird's. The body bones are solid."

"Claws . . ." she said, kneeling, focusing her light.

"Check out the fangs." He touched one of the teeth with the tip of his finger. "And the skull. The jaw reminds me of an alligator, but the top of the skull is more like a lizard. What do you estimate the length? Ten feet? Eleven? This animal must have weighed over three hundred pounds. A three-hundred-pound creature with huge legs, fangs and wings."

"A dragon," Katherine whispered. She stood. The beams of both flashlights illuminated the skeleton of an animal that had walked this cave once. Mike's arm moved around her waist.

"You're trembling."

"I'm exploding! Mike, if an animal like this existed, how could it never have been found before?"

"We'll call in experts, but quietly. We've got to keep the public from knowing about this."

"Mike! Something is down here!" She grabbed his arm. "Something alive is down here. I can feel it. Can't you?"

He answered softly. "Yes. I often feel it."

She moved closer to him in the dark. "What is it? Is it what attacked you?"

"No. Whatever attacked me was alien. Not the ghost. What you feel is the real dragon . . . or its ghost. I'm not sure I can tell the difference. But it's here."

"I can't handle this!" Katherine shuddered. "Suddenly I'm terrified!"

Mike drew her into his arms. His warmth enveloped her as he held her protectively. Katherine closed her eyes and leaned into the hardness of his chest. She hadn't known a man's body could feel so solid or so safe a shield.

"There *is* something here! How could that smell get into the cave?" she asked. "Where is it coming from?"

"It is the breath of the dragon." His fingers laced through her hair. "I'm taking you out of here."

But he didn't move. Instead, he held her so close she felt his heart beating against her cheek and the quiet heaving of his every breath in the dark silence of the cave.

He kissed her forehead. When she raised her head in surprise, his lips moved over her eyelids. He kissed each of her closed eyes and whispered her name into the silence. In a moment he was kissing her cheek, and then her lips.

A soft kiss, light, tender, yet in the touch of his lips was the most untamed passion Katherine had ever felt—his passion—contained just barely under the surface, like a current of electricity. The poet's words thundered at her like the rhythmic beats of his heart. "It is I . . . I make my way. . ." She felt herself go limp in his arms.

He was her weakness as well as her strength.

7

THEY EMERGED from the medieval dungeon into the light of a twentieth-century sun.

"Are you okay, Kathy?" he asked softly.

"Yes," she lied. "Are you?"

He smiled and circled his arm around her shoulder as they walked across the green grass of the bailey. "Don't ever be afraid when you're with me. Nothing can ever happen to you when you're with me."

She looked up at him, knowing this was true. His kiss was still with her, still heating her. Still confusing her.

He squeezed her shoulder with affection. The two spaniels scrambled out into the ward, wriggling greetings. Their feet and legs were wet from romping along the shores of the lake.

The sky had become overcast in the past hour. They looked up at the threatening clouds as if a storm was something to be expected on a day as ominous as this.

In the keep tower, Thomas had coffee and sandwiches prepared, with a bowl of fresh fruit and a tray of cookies. While they sat around the heavy oak table, Mike told his father as calmly as he could about the remarkable discovery.

Thomas was quick to grasp the situation. "The world's first evidence of a living dragon? You'll have reporters from all continents swarming over this place like hornets! Your castle inn will be a million-dollar jackpot overnight."

"That can't happen," Mike said. "I came here for a life of peace. Worldwide publicity is the last thing I want."

"Can you see it?" Katherine said. "Village shops selling dragon T-shirts and dragon beer mugs and dragon cigarette lighters made in Korea and stuffed dragon dolls wearing little Welsh hats? It'll be more sensational than Nessie."

Mike held his head and groaned. "You're right. We couldn't work, couldn't do anything. We wouldn't have a moment's peace. We can't breathe a word of this to anybody."

"But, Mike," she argued. "You know you can't keep something like this hidden. We have to know what the thing is."

Thomas said, "We'll have to get an expert to come in. It can't be disturbed until a paleontologist examines it."

Mike nodded. "That will be tricky."

"Maybe not," Katherine said. "A scientist would want this kept from the media. He wouldn't want a circus atmosphere to work in, either."

Thomas smiled. "I have a fraternity brother from Birmingham who is now on the faculty at Oxford. Lester has friends in the scientific community. He can steer us in the right direction. I'll give him a phone call." He rose and pulled on a sweater.

"There's a storm coming in," Katherine said. "I'd better leave my bicycle here and catch a ride into town with you."

"You can't leave," Mike argued. "Not now. I'm keyed up and I want your company."

"Do stay, Katherine," his father said. "Keep the lad company. I've got other errands I might as well do, so I won't be back for a while. I can give you a lift later on."

He reached for his raincoat, chuckling. "Lester and I haven't talked in twenty years. When I tell him we have a dragon, he'll think I'm phoning from an asylum."

They could hear the echo of his laughter from the stairs.

"Thanks for staying," Mike said.

"I wanted to stay. I don't want to sit alone and think about it."

"Neither do I." He pushed away from the table. "It's getting cold. I'm going to light the fire."

By the time Katherine had cleared up the dishes, the fire was blazing and Mike was slumped lazily on the sofa staring into the flames.

"You look a bit glassy eyed," she said. "Do you want more coffee? Or something stronger?"

"No. Come sit beside me."

When she did, he squeezed her hand. "I know I said it before, but I'm glad you're here. Especially now."

"So am I."

"You've brought beauty into this bleak castle, Kathy. Do you know how long it's been since I've had beauty in my life? I'd forgotten what softness was until I saw the firelight shining in your hair. Until I touched you. I didn't plan to kiss you in the cave."

"I know. I don't really understand you, Mike. Why do you deprive yourself of the company of women? You're young and attractive and every girl in the village is trying to get your attention."

"That's only a game they play. I passed the stage of kids' games long ago."

Katherine could hear this man's loneliness, but was unable to understand it. How could a man who was desired by so many women be lonely? "Yet some of these girls are beautiful," she reminded him. "And you say you long for beauty. . . ."

"For more than beauty. Companionship. That certain feeling of being really comfortable with another person. I no longer have any tolerance for all the rituals, courting games and mind games people play. You know what I mean. My hunch is you feel the same."

"Yes, I do know what you mean."

He leaned back and closed his eyes and said lazily, "Something about you gives me peace. Comfort, too."

"Well, after all, we've known each other for four years." Katherine's own words sounded hollow to her, for she hadn't known him at all, and he didn't know her. After four years of correspondence they knew almost nothing about each other. Sometimes it seemed as if he scarcely remembered her letters. The differences between the letters and the man ought to be important, yet somehow weren't. The letters were the past and this was the present and although they didn't know each other as well as they might, what did it matter, if they enjoyed each other's company for these few summer days together?

"We haven't known each other," he mumbled, eyes closed, as if he were reading her mind. "Letters aren't the same."

"Why did you write? Now that I've met you, you don't seem the letter-writing type."

"Let's not talk about the letters. Tell me about you."

"I have, in the letters."

"No, only part of you. There is another side that you don't reveal. Do you have a lover back in Allendale?"

"No. My younger sister teases me about being a spinster."

"A what?" Eyes still closed, Michael chuckled.

"You already knew that from my letters. The fire is making you sleepy. Why don't you rest for a little while?"

"That'd be despicable manners."

"Don't be silly. I don't mind. I'm perfectly happy here by the fire, and there is plenty to read."

"I don't want to sleep." He slid down until his head was resting in her lap, pulled his feet onto the long sofa and settled against her with a deep, contented sigh. Within seconds he had drifted into sleep.

Katherine smiled as she gazed down at him. The soft glow of the fire softened the features of his handsome face. She brushed the dark hair away from his eyes and rested her hand on his forehead. He didn't stir.

Touching Mike was different from touching any other man, but Katherine didn't know why. She was afraid to know why. When he had kissed her in the darkness of the cave—even the light, respectful way he kissed her—it shook loose emotions she didn't know she possessed.

As if it were the most natural thing in the world, he had fallen asleep on her lap. Katherine rested her hand on his arm, where she felt the bandage under his shirt. She watched him breathe, and studied the shadows of his eyelashes against his cheek. This was her man of letters? Letters on a college football shirt, maybe. Yet when she watched him sleep, her stomach fluttered with restless sensations she had almost forgotten.

Don't do this to me, Michael! she wanted to scream.

In the shadows of the fireflames Katherine sat thinking of the storm outside and the hideous, wildly exciting mystery hidden in the cave beneath the castle. The feel of the bandage on his arm reminded her that however dead that creature might be, there was something else down somewhere in the depths of the castle—something very much alive.

Mike continued to sleep, his head on her lap, the rhythm of his breathing even. Careful not to disturb him, Katherine turned on the table lamp beside the sofa and picked up a magazine from several that were stacked there. At her movement, Mike stirred and grasped her hand and held on tightly. This hulk of a man who had promised to guard her against all danger—this knight of the castle protecting her from the claws of a dragon—reached out to her for comfort in his sleep. To Katherine the gesture was more intimate than his kiss because it was unconscious. He had reached to her. He did not let go of her hand. Why?

The woman he'd loved—his wife—had died. In loneliness, he needed the kind of comfort only a woman could give. Had he kissed her for the same reason? No, the kiss was meant to comfort her when she was afraid.

But his kiss had not comforted her, nor did the intimate grasp of his hand in sleep. Long-suppressed needs wakened and rose to the surface and assaulted Katherine.

Don't do this to me, Michael! Even as she made the silent plea, watching Mike sleep, her fingertips, soft and trembling, touched his eyelids and his lips.

She was free. Her knight of long-ago dreams was beside her, so why was she so afraid? Because to love him meant pain. This, like all dreams, couldn't last. Mike was part of her summer, no more. There was no place in his life for her.

An hour and a half later two dogs appeared at the door with Thomas, who was carrying a sack of groceries. His gray eyebrows raised at the sight of Mike sound asleep on the lap of their guest, holding her hand in his, against his cheek.

Katherine looked up from her magazine and smiled with a little shrug. The old man shook his head incredulously and proceeded into the kitchen with his purchases. The dogs, always interested in food, followed on his heels.

In moments he was back, carrying two glasses of beer, one of which he handed to Katherine with a chuckle. "I don't believe my eyes. This is appalling."

Pembroke, always the happy one, was wagging her tail furiously. She poked her cold nose into the face of her sleeping master and began licking with devoted abandon.

Mike sputtered and stirred. Only then did his fingers release Katherine's hand. His eyes opened, saw the dog first and then his father seating himself in the opposite chair. He blinked and shot into a sitting position. "I fell asleep."

"Quite soundly asleep," Katherine said.

Wiping his mouth with his shirt sleeve, he straightened and brushed back his hair. "I'm sorry, Kathy."

"You were dead tired." She offered her beer to him, which he accepted and gulped thirstily. "Did you get hold of your friend at Oxford, Thomas?"

"It was priceless! I haven't had such fun in years. A paleontologist is on his merry way. He'll be here tomorrow."

Mike rose, stretched and went to stoke up the fire. "If he needs accommodation, it will have to be in the castle, not the village. We'll give him your room, Dad, and you can bunk with me. I hope you made it clear that the conditions of the cave are hazardous and this guy needs to be agile."

"Of course I made it clear. Lester wanted every detail. He's already named our creature 'Reese's Jolly Folly.' Isn't that a humiliating name for a dragon?"

"So he didn't believe you."

"Of course not. He's a scientist." Thomas proceeded to light his pipe, puffing vigorously. "He's also a curious man, which makes him a good scientist."

Katherine rose with a stiff back and went to the window alcove to gaze out across the lake and the sweep of hills beyond. "It looks like a bad storm," she said.

Thomas sat back, smoking. "Blasted storms. It's been storming like this for a month. The roads are like hog yards. I nearly slid into the ditch at the crossroads."

"Maybe I should have gone into the village with you."

"Why don't you stay the night, Katherine? My bed is made up fresh and like Mike said, I can bunk with him."

"Good plan," Mike agreed, kneeling at the hearth. "That way you'll be here if the paleontologist arrives early in the morning. We'll have dinner and sit around the fire and you can tell us dragon stories."

"I hate to take your bed, Thomas." Chilled by the howls and whines of the storm, Katherine turned from the window and went to sit on the floor near the hearth, next to Mike. The fire was blazing.

"Nonsense. It matters not the least to me where my old bones rest."

"Well, if you're sure. It does sound like a perfect way to spend a stormy night."

"Not quite perfect," Mike muttered for her ears alone. There was a shine in his blue eyes she hadn't seen before. Something had changed between them in the past hours, since he'd kissed her in the dragon's cave.

The closeness of those moments had not left them, and she knew now it never would.

"I can think of something more perfect for a stormy night," Mike whispered. His thigh brushed hers on the sheepskin rug by the fire. And his eyes unnerved her.

NOT ONE, BUT TWO scientists materialized before eleven in the morning. They had rushed out from England by private plane and rented a car as soon as the weather permitted. Their skepticism prevailed and they took no care to hide it. Katherine opted not to go along when Mike took the two men down into the cave, for there was little enough room to move in the rock cavity where the dragon bones lay.

The wait was excruciating. She and Thomas played horseshoes in the sunshine on the wet grass of the bailey. She rang the stake only twice in an hour, finally gave up and they played a game of ball with the dogs. The air was fresh and crisp after last night's storm, and the sky was powder blue. Birds nesting in the high ramparts of the castle chattered and fluttered noisily above them.

When the three men, carrying flashlights and small cases of instruments, emerged from the stairwell landing two hours later, lemonade and sandwiches were waiting for them on a table in the main courtyard.

"Baffling," said one, whose name was Paul. "The skeleton is an eleven-foot-long reptile, a heavy individual. The skull is unlike any I've ever seen. The wings are like those of a modern bird, but of no European species. Bones appear fossilized, but not uniformly. We'll need lab studies."

"Nothing looks or feels right," said the second man, named Darby. "If it's a hoax, it was done by people with a knowledge of the paleontological sciences."

"And with a bloody lot of money to invest," Paul said.

Darby, a small man with glasses, rubbed his chin. "These bones are reptilian, no question of that. And at least some of them are fossils."

Mike shifted restlessly. "A hoax? In a place like that? It's only by chance I ever found it."

"Anyone who understood paleontology would know a hoax could be exposed with modern technology," Katherine said.

Paul, who wore a salt-and-pepper beard, was drinking thirstily from his second glass of lemonade. "My thoughts, too. We have made records of the position, the cave conditions, everything necessary before the bones are moved. We want to transport the whole specimen. It will take several hours to do it right, so that we can reconstruct the skeleton exactly as it was found."

"Damnedest thing I ever saw," Darby mumbled.

Mike said, "I suppose I ought to mention that we have a few other odd things going on in the gatehouse. Sometimes we get a sulphur odor. It can be weak or strong enough to gag on. There are unexplained sounds. One is the clicking that legend attributes to dragon's claws moving on the stone floors, and the other, heard less often, resembles wings flapping."

"According to the stories," Katherine interjected, "these things have gone on in the castle for centuries."

The scientists looked from one to the other with such astonishment that Mike was forced to laugh. "In all fairness, since you're considering the possibility of a hoax, I ought to tell you that about a week ago my arm was slashed in the dark, near the dungeon passage—by somebody who wanted the wounds to look like three claw marks."

"Somebody? Who?"

"I couldn't see. Something knocked my flashlight out of my hands. The sulphur smell was bad at the time. My dog bit him, I think. There are bloodstains. Can you do an analysis of dried bloodstains?"

"Of course," the bearded man answered. "We'll see to that, as well. You're right, this does appear to be rather theatrical, to say the least. Were you badly injured?"

"Bad enough. The cuts got infected."

"All bloody fishy, this," said the man named Darby. "I, for one, am eager to find out what we have down there. It's a good job you've kept mum about this find, Mr. Reese."

Katherine refilled his glass. "You know, gentlemen," she said good-naturedly, "Aawn castle has been haunted by a dragon for some eight hundred years. Why is it you scientists always try your best to take the fun out of everything?"

A DAY LATER the paleontologists were gone and the remains of the dragon with them. The results would be relayed back from the lab as soon as possible.

Mike drove into the village as soon as the men left, to have his arm checked at the hospital. Afterward he showed up at Maggie Mills's house just as Katherine was finishing breakfast, lingering to visit with her landlady over a cup of tea.

He spirited Katherine to the front foyer, where he told her, "Now all we can do is wait to find out if our dragon is really a dragon. It's frustrating as hell. I've decided to take the morning off and spend it with you. Suddenly I want some time to enjoy myself. I looked at the clear skies this morning and decided this is a picnic day."

"I'd like nothing better," she said. "Let's go shopping for supplies."

"Already done. I put in an order at the bakery on my way to the hospital and picked it up on my way back. We have sandwiches with freshly baked bread, and fruit and cake. And I've brought a bottle of wine. We're all set." He led the way outside.

"Such efficiency! What's the prognosis on your arm?"

"Healing fine, thanks to you. I brought the car because Dad took the scientists and the dragon to the airport in the truck. I'm afraid it's not much of a car. Vehicles have no interest for me anymore, after spending years solely involved with them."

When they were driving, she said, "You've made a thorough effort to leave your old life behind, haven't you? Did you mean your job had something to do with cars?"

"I designed them. I came up with an electric car that was so inexpensive to run that I was offered several million dollars by the oil industry for the design, so they could destroy it. Automakers got involved in the deal, and with all the wheeling and dealing I realized the engine wasn't ever going to be manufactured. Talk about disillusionment. The rest of my life was a mess at the time, and the stress of the business world was taking its toll on my health. I said the hell with all of it, sold my design to the devil, sold my house and came over here to the real world."

UP TO 6 FREE GIFTS FOR YOU!
Look inside—all gifts are absolutely free!

If offer card is missing write to:
Harlequin Reader Service, 3010 Walden Ave., P.O. Box 1867, Buffalo, NY 14269-1867

DETACH AND MAIL CARD TODAY!

NO POSTAGE
NECESSARY
IF MAILED
IN THE
UNITED STATES

BUSINESS REPLY MAIL
FIRST CLASS MAIL   PERMIT NO. 717   BUFFALO, NY

POSTAGE WILL BE PAID BY ADDRESSEE

HARLEQUIN READER SERVICE
3010 WALDEN AVE
PO BOX 1867
BUFFALO NY 14240-9952

Behind These Doors!

GIFTS

GALORE

There's no cost— and no obligation to buy anything!

We'd like to send you free gifts to introduce you to the benefits of the Harlequin Reader Service®: free home delivery of brand-new Harlequin Temptation® novels months before they're available in stores, and at a savings from the cover price!

Accepting our free gifts places you under no obligation to buy anything ever. You may cancel the Reader Service at any time, even just after receiving your free gifts, simply by writing "cancel" on your statement or returning a shipment of books to us at our cost. But if you choose not to cancel, every month we'll send you four more Harlequin Temptation® novels, and bill you just $2.64* apiece—and there's **no** extra charge for shipping and handling. There are **no** hidden extras!

Free Gifts For You!

Look inside—Right Now!
We've got something
special just for you!

"A very rich man, as a result."

"Believe me, it takes a rich man to do what I'm trying to do. By the time we finish renovating the castle, I'll be poor. But I'll be happy."

"You never wrote about any of that," she said. "You never really explained why you decided to come to Wales, except that you had retired from corporate stress."

They had passed the outskirts of the village. The gray slate roofs were behind them, and ahead stretched fertile valleys and the moorlands.

"It's understandable, of course," Katherine continued. "You wanted to get away from your past, so you wouldn't be inclined to discuss it in letters. Actually, you're an excellent writer. I always thought you should try your hand at fiction."

"I'm heavily into fiction at the moment," he said sourly.

"What do you mean?"

"Pay no attention. You perceive me as a straightforward person, and I'm not. I'm devious. I'm a lie disguised as a man."

She gazed hard at him. His face was strangely blank. "What the devil are you talking about?"

He sighed shakily, unwilling to look at her. "Oh, hell, I just . . . can't . . ." He paused. "I'm not what you expected. . . . You had other impressions, I know that. . . ."

"False impressions, you mean? Yes, you are different from what I expected. I thought you were much more . . . leisurely and laid-back. Your ambition for the castle, which I see now is a real drive, didn't come through. You seemed . . . much older than you are. I imagined you near the age of retirement, certainly not in your early twenties."

"I'm not in my early twenties. I'm twenty-eight."

"Are you? You don't look it."

"I can't be more than a year or two younger than you."

"Even at twenty-eight, you're almost eight years younger."

"Yeah? I guessed wrong on that."

Katherine hurried to change the subject. "Will the swans be on the river?"

"Yep. I made sure we have extra bread to feed them."

Twenty-eight, she thought. Could he be telling the truth? He must be, because a man any younger could hardly have a past like his—a marriage that ended when his wife died, and a short, incredible career in the auto design industry that left him a millionaire. From the way he talked, he considered the two of them contemporaries. But she, in her mid-thirties, had not imagined herself with a man so young. Katherine Glenn of Fielding College could not imagine herself with a man like this. But it was summer now and Allendale was far away. It was a magical summer, when she could let herself be honest enough to admit she felt as young as he.

Because feeling young was not the same as being young, she had been afraid to face a growing, unsettling attraction for Mike . . . until he kissed her. What did it matter—all that social conditioning she had fought all her life? Mike had kissed her the way no man ever had.

HE SPREAD A BLANKET in the shadows of low-hanging branches. The shadows barely moved in the late-morning air, for there was no wind. Sunlight designed bright patches on the grass, through the leaves. The river gurgled its little song as it moved, but in its wide, reedy shallows, the water was barely rippling. The swans swam leisurely, and a dozen ducks floated along the water's edge, next to the grassy bank. Above, birds offered their musical talents to the splendor of the summer morning.

Katherine, dressed in a light wool skirt and a white silk blouse, stretched out her legs and leaned back on her elbows, lifting her face to the sun. "It's lovely," she said. "I'll never forget this place . . . this day."

"Or the man who is here beside you? Tell me you won't forget me, Kathy."

"How could I? How could I, ever?"

He moved his fingers slowly down the length of her arm. "These are the kinds of moments one wishes could last so long that there would be no question of forgetting them."

"We don't remember days, or even hours," she said softly. "We remember moments."

"This moment . . ." Mike's blue eyes met hers with such adoration her heart trembled. His lips moved over hers, gently at first, like the kiss in the darkness of the cave. Then less gently. He caught his arms around her as she began to fall backward, and he held her and fell back with her onto the soft cushion of grass. His kiss grew deeper, warmer, openmouthed, hungry.

8

FLOATING ON THE sensations of his kiss, Katherine could no longer feel the soft earth under them. The fluffy clouds overhead seemed close enough to touch. She lost herself in the man who held her. Time whirled away on illusions that she and Mike had been here before, long, long ago, centuries ago, and had never left. It seemed, in those untamed moments, as if for a hundred centuries she had known him and in all that time nothing had ever changed—not the whispering river or the slow dance of swans or the dewdrops on bracken, or the flitting of yellow butterflies over purple wildflowers.

Or the feel of Michael's body against her own.

He raised over her, balancing on one elbow, and stroked her auburn hair as she lay against the grass. "You're beautiful. When I'm around you, I want to touch you. It takes all my discipline not to. It's driving me insane, the way I want to touch you."

"I don't understand...us," she muttered, looking up into his eyes.

"What do you mean, you don't understand us? It's something that has been going on in the world for quite some time now—the passion between man and woman."

"But we're . . . so different, Michael."

"Different from each other? Sure, we are. Anything wrong with that?" He touched her breast over the silk of her blouse. "Your heart is beating as wildly as mine. That is what we have in common."

She lay very still, looking up at him, her tousled hair flowing against the grass. Her face felt flushed; her heartbeats were out of control. Mike did not lift his hand from her breast. His fingers moved as lightly as feathers.

"I don't scare you, do I?" he whispered.

"I don't think so," she lied.

"Ah, but I do. I'm too impulsive. I don't mean to be. I can't help myself. I'm too conscious of an awful, temporary feeling, because time won't stand still. You'll slip through my fingers and be gone."

"But this . . . will only make it worse," she said, and her voice was filled with sadness.

He heaved a great sigh. "I can't think rationally. I don't even want to try to think. The first minute I saw you, I knew I was in trouble. My whole system sprang into alert."

She reached up and touched his face. The alert she understood, because she was experiencing one right now, all through her body. His deep kiss had started the alarm, and the tingling wouldn't stop. And his eyes . . . how seductive his eyes were!

"Mike . . ." She held his face in both her hands, looking up at him, luxuriating in the beauty of him, unable to believe a man who looked like this was speaking heartfelt love words meant for her. *Oh, God, what is he seeing in my eyes?*

He lowered his lips to hers again, convincing her, in the intensity of his kiss, that this was the first kiss of her life. His hand moved over her breasts, caressing through thin layers of silk and lace. Her fingers moved through his thick, dark hair. He roused her as if she were emerging from a long sleep, and Katherine was suddenly wildly alive, her body quaking in the rush of the wakening needs. She surrendered to the wakening—and tensed with an unbearable ache of wanting. Of wanting him.

It can't be! a warning voice within her screamed.

She sat up suddenly. "Mike! What are we doing?"

Gently he reached to pick a leaf of grass from her hair. "I'd say what we're doing is . . . getting better acquainted."

She swallowed and looked away. "Just how acquainted do you plan for us to get?"

Mike's smile was more tender than she had ever seen it as he took her hand in his. "Honey, I'm not planning. I'm just acting on my impulses. I'll back off if you want. The last thing I want is to threaten you. If I did, I'm sorry."

"You wanted to find out what my—my reactions would be to your . . . impulses. . . ."

"Guilty as charged. I did want to know. I wanted you yourself to know." He was outlining her lips with the tip of his finger as he talked. "Now we both know."

"You're confusing me."

"Good. That means you're not locked into some stiff, preconceived ideas."

"You're awfully sure of yourself," she said softly.

He sat back. "Is that how I seem? Sure of myself? Not here, Kathy. Not with you." He picked pensively at the grass. "Damn, there is so little time. How can I know what to do when there is so little time?"

Her throat constricted. She closed her eyes.

He was so hard to read, she thought. No, that wasn't true; he was easy to read. The hard part was believing what was happening. "I have another three weeks in Wales."

He smiled. "Yeah. Why can't I look on the bright side like you do? We'll take each day as it comes. Honey, there is such confusion in your eyes. I know this is fast. I've never been a patient guy when I . . . when I want something."

"Maybe I'm the same," she answered. "What the hell? Life is exciting with you! Shall we open that bottle of wine?"

"Yes," he said as he bent down and kissed her eyelids.

They had this, at least, she thought—and they would live for the beauty of each moment, trying to forget their days together were limited to the length of her vacation.

This day—their day—was more dream than real. They picked wildflowers along the riverbank and fed the ducks and swans. While they ate their picnic lunch, a fat hedgehog moved out of a thicket of bramble bushes and scampered into a fallen log. At the slightest excuse Mike would kiss her playfully and tell her his heart was captured for all and forever. There was nothing to connect the day to any other that had ever been, or ever would be again.

When a chill descended from the late-afternoon sky, they gathered up the picnic remains and shook the grass from the blanket and from themselves. Katherine combed her hair and made an attempt at repairing her makeup. Mike borrowed her comb. After the car was loaded up, he opened the passenger door for her and bent to kiss her once more before she got into the car.

"Kathy," he said. "Make no mistake. I want you. In a way I've never wanted a woman, I want you."

THE REPORT FROM the paleontologists was disappointing and horrifying. Katherine had torn open the seal and unfolded a typewritten letter three pages long. "Thank heaven they've put this in laymen's terms for us," she said, and proceeded to read the report. "'The bones are those of a Komodo dragon, a living lizard inhabiting Indonesia. The skull has been tampered with. Part of the jawbone and some teeth are identified as Australian crocodile. And the wing bones belong to a species of African vulture.'"

She looked up. "Can you believe this?"

"A hoax!" Mike blurted. "The thing is a deliberate hoax!"

"A lizard eleven feet long?" Thomas asked.

"How on earth could this be?" Katherine asked. "I've seen Komodo dragons in a California zoo. They're absolutely hideous, and they eat large animals, even humans. And you're right, Mike, this report confirms that they weigh around three hundred pounds." She scowled. "A Japanese lizard? Somebody actually—" She stopped and looked down at the trembling paper in her hands. "The letter goes on. 'Some of the bones are fossils. These bones were painstakingly placed among the others, which have undergone some kind of chemical process that makes them appear as fossils to the naked eye.'"

"Damn!" Mike swore, his voice husky with disappointment, his teeth clenched in anger. "Somebody has gone to one hell of a lot of trouble to create a dead dragon!"

"Trouble and expense!" She waved the letter. "They say that procuring and processing these bones and fitting this hoax together must have cost fifty thousand pounds. Experts were involved." She handed the type-written pages to Mike.

"For what possible motive?" Thomas asked as he attempted to light his pipe.

"To drive the two of you out?" Katherine suggested.

"What? With a pile of bones?"

"To convince you dragons are real."

"Bosh and slop," Thomas said. "Dragons real? Can't be that."

Mike was looking over the remainder of the letter. "The results of the blood analysis aren't back yet." He rubbed his forehead as if it ached. "I think we can assume that whoever would go to these lengths to create a fossil of a dragon would also go to whatever trouble and expense was necessary to simulate a live dragon in the castle."

"And even attack you," Katherine agreed. "But *why?*"

"I've had enemies before," Thomas said. "Enemies I could identify and understand and deal with. But this . . ."

Mike rose from his chair. "I'll get them," he swore. "I intend to find out who did this and why!"

Katherine tried to draw her emotions inside herself. She had seen the bones of a dragon and believed what she had seen, because the concept of a hoax seemed too farfetched. In the cave she had felt the presence of something not human; she was certain the phantom was near. Mike knew, too. He was telling the truth when he told her the dragon still lurked within the castle, if only as a restless ghost.

"Have you seen anyone around the gatehouse?" Katherine asked. "How can a prankster get in without being seen?"

"I can't figure it," Mike said on his way to the kitchen. "The inner passage leads into the bailey. All the openings come off the bailey—there's no other way in or out."

He returned chewing on one of the pastries Katherine had brought out that morning. "I feel like killing whoever did this! How dare anybody mess with my castle . . . and make a mockery of my dragon!"

"Your dragon?" his father asked.

"Yeah, mine! Kathy's and mine!" He hit a fist against his palm. "I need to get out and try to vent some frustration. Do you feel like going for a short drive, Kathy?"

"Sure. Where?"

"The hills. I can think better in the hills."

THE TRUCK BOUNCED up a road that was little more than a sheep's trail. When they reached a high plateau Mike stopped, got out and went around to open the door for her. They stood looking back on a view of the village and the towers of the Castle of Aawn. The moors stretched before them on either side—lush grasslands blown by wind and grazed by long-tailed sheep. Hills alive with legends from centuries past, legends of ghosts and dragons that refused to die.

"I need to run," he said. "Do you mind waiting a few minutes for me?"

"Of course not."

He took off in a sprint across the moors. Katherine watched until he disappeared over the crest of a small hill. Then she began to walk, feeling the wind in her hair and the sun on her face, understanding Mike's desire to be out here where everything was wild and without boundaries. It gave a sense of freedom. The hills were so old and so unchanged. So free of the insanity of civilization and the perverted motives of misguided men who perpetrated hoaxes upon others. The cold wind was cleansing. Revitalizing.

Time was lost here because there was no way to calculate it, so Katherine had no idea how much time elapsed before Mike appeared again, still running at a good pace. Some fifty meters from the car he spotted her.

He rushed up, twirled her around in his arms and pulled her to the ground on top of him. Panting hard from the run, he lay on the grass, holding her. Neither spoke.

They lay still, with only the sound of his heavy breathing and the sound of the wind in the grass. Soon there was only the sound of the wind.

Then the sensations of his kiss. Again. Mike said, "You are affecting my work and my sleep. I can't think about anything but you. Tell me, lovely lady, are you sleeping as soundly as before you met me?"

"That's an incriminating question."

"Aha! It wouldn't be incriminating if the answer wouldn't incriminate! So you do think about me in the night."

"Yes." *How can I help it?* she thought. *How could any woman help it?*

"I thought so. I hoped so."

His lips drew close again, and as always when he kissed her, the kiss took reality away with it, took time away. Her response this time was less surrender than acceptance. Acceptance of him.

There was no point denying what she felt for Mike— not to herself, not to him. She was unable to analyze the wisdom of her feelings when he was this close and his lips were on hers and his body was hard and warm beneath her.

Her name came whispered on the wind. "Beautiful lady... you're becoming my obsession."

His hand moved under her sweater to caress her full breasts over the lace of her bra. "There is nothing softer in the world," he mumbled. "Kiss me, Kathy...."

His lips opened under hers, moved with hers. She fell under the spell of him, which was a spell of magic, a spell she could not fight and no longer wanted to fight.

His solid body was pure masculine strength and beauty to her. She ran her hand along his shoulders and his back as he kissed her. As he caressed her. Closing her eyes, Katherine rode the waves of passion that lifted her to a dimension she hadn't known in her life. There was no coming down from this, she was certain—not today, nor tomorrow, nor ever.

"Kathy, say you want me."

"I do want you..." a voice that was scarcely her own whispered back.

His answer was an impassioned moan that came from deep in his throat. "My lady..." He brushed her blowing hair from her face. "This wind is too cold to caress your body. Only I can do that. I'm more gentle than the wind. And only I can keep you warm. The ground is hard and an hour from now the air will begin to chill. I don't want to share you with the circling hawk up there or with the bleating sheep, or even with the wind. Let me take you to the comfort of my bed."

She looked down into his eyes. The images inspired by the poet's words rushed back with the force of a tidal wave, sweeping over her. "I am stern, acrid, large, undissuadable, but I love you..." She trembled violently. *Love*, Katherine thought. *I don't know what it is. Is it this ache that overpowers and controls?*

He hugged her tightly. "Your eyes say yes."

"What will your father think if I . . . if we . . . ?"

He didn't answer at once. "He'll have to think we are deeply enamored of each other and he'd be right."

"I'd hate for him to think less of me, but of course he would understand that it isn't as if we'd just met. I mean, we've known each other for years, and I did come here because of you. Your father knows all that. He isn't too strictly old-fashioned, is he?"

"I don't—I don't think so. . . ."

"Is something wrong? Your father—"

"My father understands me very well. He knows I've asked no other woman to Aawn—to my bed—and he respects you. Stay the night with me. When the castle is quiet and he is asleep, then lie with me. The night will belong to us."

Insects were humming songs around the scattered flowers. The smell of wild grass was sweet. In the distance sheep bleated mournfully. Small clouds danced in front of the sun. The peace was profound, but their bodies were not at peace.

Mike shifted restlessly. "These tight jeans weren't made for trysts with you. They're killing me."

Katherine rose quickly to her feet. "Maybe a race to the car will bring your temperature down." She was already sprinting away from him, and he had to move fast to catch up.

THAT LATE AFTERNOON she helped with the building in the Great Hall, welcoming a chance to share in the manifestation of Mike's dream. The glass installation in the windows was completed. Workmen were busy with electrical wiring and the running of water pipes. Mike was doing cabinet-frame work in the alcove where a kitchen was to be installed, just below his small kitchen on the level above. Katherine helped with leveling and some sanding, and sweeping up sawdust that was causing some of the floor stones to be slippery.

As she envisioned the finished room she began to absorb the excitement of the project. Little of the original atmosphere was being sacrificed.

Thomas prepared a fine dinner of roast pork, new potatoes and baked onions. Cooking was his recent endeavor and he was justly proud of his efforts. Katherine, who had little interest in cooking, was grateful that Thomas consistently refused her offers to help. Mike, by contrast, was pleased when she wanted to work with him in the Great Hall.

At dinner Mike's eyes never left her, and he was so attentive that Thomas could not fail to notice.

Everything Katherine had previously experienced and believed about men, Mike made a myth of. Like the myth that wild, spontaneous coupling—as might have come about on the moors this afternoon—was splendor at its highest. Mike had lit every hidden fire in her and then prolonged the anticipation for them both. With each hour the heat grew, fanned by the flames of his exquisite attention.

She could feel his sexual energy filling the space between them, and when he came near her it became so powerful that Katherine struggled to maintain her composure, for the sake of Thomas. At the least opportunity, Mike would touch her, softly on the hand, or a slight brush against her shoulder. Each touch was like igniting a match.

He could have made love to her on the moors, but he chose this way instead. It was his way of showing her that lying together was not spontaneous play, but an act to be anticipated and remembered. It made the evening almost unbearable. She felt cold and then hot, sat by the fire and then moved away. Sometimes she didn't dare look at Mike for fear of giving her thoughts away. Other times, no power on earth could make her turn her eyes from him.

At last Thomas yawned. "These old bones are finished for the day. Are you staying the night again, Katherine, dear? You must. It's getting late. I'll just haul myself up to Michael's lair."

Katherine felt a blush redden her cheeks. She opened her mouth to speak without the faintest idea what to say, but Mike spoke first.

"Dad," he said evenly, "take your own bed tonight. If Kathy decides to stay, there's room upstairs for her."

Thomas set his pipe in the ashtray. He looked from one to the other with an expression Katherine could not identify. It was a kind of wistfulness that made her uneasy.

"Well," he said. The word jammed with a rasp. He cleared his throat and began again. "Well, good night, then."

"Good night, Thomas," she said softly.

The old man smiled at her and glanced at his son, who was sitting on the floor in front of Katherine's chair, leaning against her legs. Thomas's eyes hardened then, as if he were giving Mike a warning. Mike met his eyes and said nothing as he rested his arm on her knees protectively.

When they were alone Mike drew a screen across the fireplace and picked up the bottle of sherry. "Do you mind carrying the glasses? I need a hand free for the flashlight."

The pitch-black, winding stairwell felt ice-cold with the night wind pushing in through the arrowloops. Partway up, Katherine stopped. "Do you hear something?"

"The wind," he said.

"Something else. I thought I heard a faint clicking. It seems to be gone now. But I have this strong feeling we're not alone. It's the same feeling I had in the dungeon!"

"The dragon, I suppose," he said softly.

"The ghost? Do you mean the ghost?"

"Honey, it won't hurt you. The sounds could be the wind through the arrowloops. Perhaps birds nesting in the slits."

She grasped his arm tightly. "Now you are patronizing me! And not answering me, not wanting to admit something is here when we both know it is! Is it the ghost of the dragon?" She had stopped dead still, listening to clicks and windlike whishes that were barely audible, but audible, nevertheless. It was as if when they rounded the next twist of the stairs, they would be closer to it, perhaps even upon it. She held tightly to the arm of the man whom she could barely see in the darkness. "Mike, what have you seen in this castle?"

He cleared his throat. "I think you've picked the worst possible place to ask me that, haven't you? Do you expect me to say, on these dark stairs, where with one slip we could fall to our death, that a ghost is in this tower?" He was trying to lighten his tone, but there was something mysterious in his voice that rode on the darkness like the ghost itself.

"I wouldn't be afraid of it," she insisted.

He was urging her up the stairway toward his apartment. "You're already afraid of it. Who wouldn't be?"

A cold breeze swirled down through the stone tower, as if the top of the fortress had reached out and caught the wind and gulped it down in one enormous breath. Katherine shivered. "It's so cold!"

Mike answered, "I'll have you a fire built in no time."

They reached a landing with a wooden door hung with giant hinges—a door too low to walk through without ducking. The stairs continued on to the wind-blown battlements. Mike opened the heavy door and motioned her inside. They stepped into darkness. He switched on a lamp.

Katherine gasped at her first sight of Mike's private apartment. In the center of the room an enormous round bed hung on chains from the ceiling beams. It was covered with furs and half a dozen pillows. Two round tables also hung on chains. On one table were two radios and on the other a portable tape recorder and a camera. A fireplace exactly like the one on the level below dominated one round wall. There were no chairs in the room, just two wooden benches placed near the hearth. Books were strewn about, and in an alcove some clothes were hanging. Mike made straight for the fireplace and began piling in kindling.

"This room!" she said. "Talk about a medieval castle!"

"Like it? I had to have furniture so I threw it together the easiest way. All I needed was plywood and a good saw and a drill and chains. I like the medieval effect."

"A round bed?"

"It wasn't planned. It was rectangular to begin with but I kept bashing myself black-and-blue on the corners so I rounded it. Looks better, anyhow. Romantic as hell, right?" He set a heavy log on the grate and lit a match to the paper and kindling underneath. "You're the first woman who has ever been up here."

"Honestly?"

"Believe it." He rose and took her in his arms. "A guy knows a princess when he's lucky enough to meet one."

"Mike . . ." she said hesitantly. "From my letters you know I'm not . . . involved with anyone. Not sexually. . . ."

"Which means you have no reason to be protected."

"Exactly."

"It's okay, honey, don't be concerned. I think I can find something. Just give me a couple seconds."

He disappeared into the alcove in which he had installed an almost-modern bathroom, and in a moment he was back.

"You're shivering. It's still cold as the devil in here. Take a while to warm this room. Come on, I'll warm you." He pulled down a fur cover. Another was underneath.

Katherine kicked off her shoes and crawled in between the layers of fur. With their movements, the bed swayed on its hinges, rocking them. She snuggled into his arms.

"Ah . . ." he said. "In a minute this will be perfect."

He wriggled out of his sweater and his shirt, bent to pull off his socks and caressed her leg with his bare feet while he slipped her sweater over her head. The thick furs were very light to move under. Mike struggled out of his jeans before he helped Katherine out of hers.

When both were naked, he pulled her into his arms with a great sigh of pleasure. "Now," he said. "It's perfect!"

The sensation of their bodies touching, linked together full-length between soft layers of fur, was a new physical sensation for Katherine. The bed moved gently, causing the chains to creak. The cold, firelit room surrounded them but couldn't touch them. Nothing in the world could touch them here. They had each other.

His hands moved over her shoulders and her back and her hips as he held her against his body. His skin was cool and warm at the same time. His body was solid muscle. His hands were gentle, luxuriating in the softness of her breasts. Her hands explored the shape of his body, the feel of his body—the slight bristle of his whiskers against her face, the pulse beating in his neck, the expanse of his shoulders, the mat of hair on his chest, the hardness of his thighs.

He slid over onto his back. "Touch me," he whispered. In the thick breath of his voice she heard his unspoken plea—*claim me . . . take possession of me.*

There was no touch more intimate. Nor possessive. There was no drawing away from it, not tonight, not ever. He moaned softly under her caress, closed his eyes and allowed himself to be carried away, subdued body and soul by her sorcery. He found her breasts again and kissed them hungrily, tasting the sweetness, drinking the softness.

The cover slid from her shoulders. With her hair falling about her face, Katherine gazed down into blue eyes that shone like ice and fire. The eyes met hers and held. His hand grasped hers, and held. For a long, silent moment, time stilled. It was a moment for absorbing and declaring love newly found without the encumbrance of words.

The flickering shadows engulfed them. The popping of burning logs made an ancient chant. Mike released his grasp on her hand. Gently, in the magical swaying of the bed, he eased her over and kissed her deeply. His hand began to explore more boldly than before... stroking her, not teasingly now, but tantalizingly. Passionately. Possessively.

Helpless and tingling, Katherine, floating on the cloudlike softness of fur, moved against the intense, seductive touch, moaning now. Writhing. And still his lips and tongue burned on hers and would not let her go. He was taking her to the most agonizing heights of passion, moving his hand firmly and gently and mercilessly.

The second before her passion exploded, Mike moved over her and into her. His giving and his taking merged, became one and the same. Katherine shuddered violently and clasped onto his shoulders as if for her life... grasping far beyond control, beyond imagination, beyond her understanding of herself, or of love.

Mike's release came with a moan uncaged from the deepest part of him. Her heart caught his helpless cry and pulled it inside herself, and the sound shuddered in her like a match flame igniting the fire all over again. Flames leaped in her loins again, and she gasped. He stayed with her until her trembling ceased.

And even longer. He stayed until his body sagged and relaxed against hers, its energy spent. Then, aware of his weight, he slid over on his side, one leg over hers and an arm over her waist. She felt his still-heavy breathing, and turned toward him.

The shine had not left his eyes. He smiled dreamily. "You're the most beautiful woman I've ever known," he whispered. "I've never felt so deeply for another person."

"You've just taken me to a place I've never been," she whispered back. "I've never felt like this, either."

He kissed her.

She touched his forehead. "You're perspiring."

"I'm hot." He threw off the cover. It slid to the floor.

The room was still cool in contrast to the steamy cocoon they had lain in, but the fire had taken off the chill. Mike's overheated body, still pressed against hers, was all the warmth she needed.

He made some adjustments to the pillows. Katherine raised on one elbow and looked around to convince herself she wasn't dreaming, but the tower room, too, was the stuff of dreams. Orange fireflames flickered on their bodies, illuminating the shine of perspiration on Mike's skin. She drank in the beauty of him. The sensation returned that she had lain with him before . . . in a castle, long, long ago. Her childhood daydream or a splinter of a memory?

Soon his breathing slowed and she felt him relax against her. He closed his eyes.

Wide awake, still tingling from his love, Katherine stared into the dancing flames of the fire. How could a man like Michael love her? A man so young, so beautiful? A man whose attentions other women would kill for?

His life was so different from hers and so far away from hers. She and Mike didn't have the things in common she had once believed they had. In reality, she scarcely knew him. She ached at the thought that she would never know him well. They had so little time.

When Michael was gone, every dream she had ever known would be gone with him.

9

MIKE WAS IN TURMOIL. A man determined to control his own life, his own world, his own destiny, he was facing circumstances that had sprouted just beyond his reach, as if his life was suddenly overrun by tangles of roses and thorns.

Katherine was the rose. Delicate and beautiful, a wild rose that had appeared so unexpectedly out of the mist. Illusive. He was unsure where she had come from or why she had come, but she would not stay. Their time was destined to be short.

Katherine was happy in the life she had chosen for herself, he was sure. To be around her was to know she was happy. She lived in intellectual surroundings. With lifelong friends. In a warm home with all the modern comforts. His home was a cold medieval fortress. It housed a dragon.

Even if she would stay, he could not be sure the thing would tolerate her presence. One of the best-known legends of the dragon of Aawn had to do with the beast's jealousy over its lords' wives. The fortress was a haven for warriors—savagely fierce fighting men who proved their worth by not cowering to the monster who dwelled within. Ladies were not welcome in the dragon's lair. None who ever lived here, according to legend, had stayed past three full moons. Women fled in terror.

Mike had recalled the legend several times since Katherine had arrived. It bothered him, because every legend grew from some basis of truth. Legends were harmless enough, but the fact remained that the dragon was still in the castle. Not matter how he felt about Katherine, he could never ask her to stay.

The dragon was one thing. This hoax was quite another. Confirmation that the dragon skeleton was a hoax had fanned the flames of his fury to the point where he could no longer concentrate on his work. Mike's anger over the invasion and deception drove him into the bottom of the gatehouse tower again, a decision he afterward bitterly regretted.

He was loading plumbing fixtures onto a chain lift outside the keep—heavy or bulky equipment was lifted up from outside rather than taken up the steep, winding stairway—when he caught the faint smell of sulphur again, from the direction of the gatehouse arches. The dragon's breath had reeked out in daytime only once before, on a day after a rising full moon. Like today.

The dragon or someone pretending to be the dragon was in the tower. With flashlight and a long-bladed knife he headed toward the gatehouse, the dogs at his heels. They seemed to sense danger and his anger, and the mixture called forth their canine hunting instincts. The dogs proceeded down like warriors off to battle. By the time Mike was winding his way through the dungeon passage, his two companions were too far ahead to be seen.

Suddenly a shrill yelp pierced the black silence, followed by ferocious barking. Mike lunged forward through the narrow hall. He caught up with the dogs at the cave entrance, where they stood barking into the cavern like two crazed banshees. No sign of anything alive appeared in the beam of light as he shone the flashlight about in every direction. The light melted into blackness in front of him.

Outside the cave entry was a pile of eight small, round river stones. Legend had linked stone gathering and stone eating to dragons for hundreds of years. Pembroke, whimpering moved into his light beam, trailing blood. Her left upper thigh was soaked red. Mike fell onto his knees beside her.

Stiff with rage, he examined the wound. It was bleeding badly, but did not appear to be deep. A knife slash, from the looks of it. Another slash across the withers was only a flesh wound. Talbot was still screaming at some unseen presence, hidden in the cave. His barks echoed from the walls.

"Come on, Talbot! We're going up!"

Still emitting growls and yips, the dog turned and obeyed his master.

Pembroke was limping. When they reached the winding stairs, Mike set down the flashlight and picked up the dog and carried her. This meant they had to ascend without benefit of light. He felt each step with his toe and ran his foot along the edge to determine where it was broken. It was a laborious trek to reach ground level and the light of day.

At Pembroke's slow pace, Mike made his way across the bailey to the gatehouse. It was lucky no workmen were in the yard, because he didn't want to have to explain how or where his dog was injured.

Thomas was in the living-room area painting an antique cabinet when Mike came off the stairs carrying the dog. His shirt was soaked through with blood.

"My God! What's happened?" The older man struggled to his feet.

"The dragon again...." Mike, after the long climb with Pembroke in his arms, was too winded to elaborate, but more detailed explanation, for the moment, was unnecessary.

Together they examined and disinfected the wounds.

"I thought this might need stitches," Mike said. "But now that we've got a better look, I'm sure it'll heal all right if we keep it clean." He patted the white head. "It's okay, girl. You'll be fine. I think her trembling was fear rather than pain. Damn, if only the dogs could talk!"

"This dragon thing has gone too far," Thomas said.

"I've had it, Dad. I'm going to flush that guy out if I have to use grenades!"

Thomas was applying disinfectant while Mike held the wriggling animal against his chest. "These are serious threats, Mike, or else it's some giant animal."

"Down there? What? A giant bat? Come on, Dad. We know the skeleton was planted by somebody."

"But we don't know when. For all we know the hoax has lain there for a century."

"Right, we don't know. But we're going to find out!"

Thomas frowned. "When you lose your temper you lose your sense with it. At some point we are going to be forced to call in the police, and this might be that point."

"It'll be public knowledge if we do. London tabloids will have a field day with this. I don't think I could take it."

His father repeated, "There might be no other choice."

Mike slammed his fist into his palm. "Hell!" He went to get himself a glass of water in the kitchen. "I didn't see a blasted thing down there. Not a thing."

Thomas returned to his painting. He sat on the floor on spread newspapers to complete the coat of paint on the oak cabinet. "We've been assuming that this . . . creature will confine itself to the gatehouse," he said. "Suppose it doesn't, though? It could go anywhere in the castle. Suppose somebody gets seriously hurt or even killed?"

"You mean Katherine. She wanders all over this castle by herself. I agree with you that it's too dangerous for her to continue to do that. I'll have a talk with her about it."

Thomas drew into an uncomfortable silence. Mike slumped onto the rug beside Pembroke and began stroking her head.

His father finally said, "Speaking of Katherine, Mike, just what the hell do you think you're doing?"

"I wondered if you were going to confront me about it."

"Wondered? You knew good and well I'd confront you. I've suspected for days that you and Katherine were attracted to each other, but I didn't expect it to go so far as your sleeping together. I've seen the effects before of your charm on women, but I thought you were more of a gentleman than to work them on a woman like Katherine. Frankly, I don't know how you did it."

A shadow crossed Mike's eyes. "You make it sound like I'm manipulating her. I'm not. I've never been so taken with a woman in my life. If I were the type to allow myself to ever fall in love again, I'd be in big trouble."

Thomas scowled. "So would she, it appears."

"You don't approve. At first I wondered if it would be a problem for you—because she was your lady, so to speak, but I've watched you closely and I know you pretty well. I don't think you're enamored. You're not, are you?"

"I thought I was before she came. But as it turns out, she isn't the type of woman for me, after all. I don't mean just because I'm too old for her. I mean, she has a spirit I wasn't aware of. Katherine has a wild streak in her, something that shuns convention. There was no hint of it in her letters. You have the same streak in you, which is what draws you to each other, I suppose, in spite of the difference in your ages."

Mike gazed hard at his father. "I've been trying to define that wild thing in Katherine. You've felt it, too, then. What is it?"

"From what she wrote, I gather Katherine was raised by wealthy parents in a small town where her father was admired, looked up to. Conventional respectability was drilled into her." Thomas smoothed the last few strokes of white paint and set his brush in a jar of thinner. He pounded on the top of the paint can to make it tight. "I think Katherine responded to her upbringing by living an exemplary life-style, when deep inside she never really gave a damn what people thought. The wild streak isn't a streak. It's the real person, allowed to surface only sometimes." He grinned at his son. "Does that remind you of anyone?"

Mike did not return the smile. He was concentrating on his father's comparison of the two of them—himself and Kathy. "Yeah. I had to find a place where I could be me. Kathy has moments of letting go here, Dad. But then she sometimes seems to...want to back away...."

"What do you expect? She found a complete stranger. She doesn't know what to make of you."

Mike felt the impact of this truth. They had played a rotten trick on her. He had tried to tell her so a dozen times, and each time he'd thought of the sadness in his father's eyes and the agony of humiliation, and the consequences of what Thomas would consider betrayal. "The worst part is living with a lie," Mike said. "You're asking more than you have a right to ask. You're being selfish as hell."

Thomas's shoulders sagged. He sighed noisily, then straightened into stiff defiance. "At this point, it's too late to reverse it. Telling her now would be stupid, because she'd hate you for letting it go on so long. I can't see what's so horrible about it. If Katherine is happier thinking you wrote to her instead of me, what great harm is done?"

"It's wrong as hell and you know it."

"But what harm?"

"I don't . . . know . . . exactly. . . ."

Thomas was cleaning paint from his hands. The unpleasant smell of turpentine and paint filled the room. "I never dreamed it would turn out like this, but now that it has, what do you intend to do about it?"

"About what?"

"About Katherine, idiot! Is this just a summer fling? And with the end of her visit, that will be the end of it?"

Mike's eyes clouded with despair. "I guess so. I couldn't ask her to stay, even if I thought she would, which she wouldn't. Even if this castle wasn't haunted and dangerous, it isn't fit for a lady. Especially in winter."

"I agree. You couldn't ask her to stay and she wouldn't, anyway. Katherine is devoted to her career.

She probably has a man in her life, although she never wrote about him. A man who wears a business suit every day and sends her roses paid for with a credit card number he has committed to memory."

"If you're trying to depress me, you're doing a great job of it."

"Just being realistic. She may have a wild streak, but she also has a life of her choosing, and it couldn't be more opposite from yours." Thomas went to the bathroom to wash his hands, came out drying them, and reached for his pipe. "Well, I suppose there's nothing wrong with a summer fling. I've had the impression from her lack of correspondence in another summer that she's had flings before. She'll be leaving in another week. But I've been watching you, lad. You never take your eyes off her. I hope you know what you're doing."

"I care for her a lot. I'm not kidding myself, if that's what you mean. When she leaves, I'll sulk around in a blue funk and you'll have to put up with it for weeks."

"Don't expect my sympathy. You did this to yourself. You could have restrained your lust and not drawn her into your lair. I don't blame her, I blame you entirely. Katherine will probably refer to it henceforth as her Wales adventure or her castle adventure, something like that. If you fell under her spell, you should have had sense enough to protect yourself."

"The wise one has spoken," Mike said.

"I don't know why I waste my breath. You have never listened to me in your life."

The bell rang. It was a bell attached to the side of the door, downstairs, with an electrical cord that extended down the stairwell to the entry. Mike rose in response. "Are you expecting a delivery?"

"Yes, from the butcher and the cheese shop."

Pembroke, who usually followed Mike, thumped her tail in protest at his leaving and rested her head on the floor.

"I'll be back, girl," he said.

It was not a grocery delivery. Mike surfaced again a couple of minutes later with an envelope. "It's our lab report," he said, tearing it open. He stood dead still, reading in silence, with his brow wrinkled into a deep frown.

"Well?" Thomas asked impatiently.

"The blood sample they took at the location where I was attacked in the keep." Mike looked at his father, then back to the paper in disbelief. "The blood is reptilian."

"STAY WITH ME for the time we have left," Mike said to Katherine over dinner at the small restaurant that joined the village pub. "I can't stand the thought of you in the village and me out there. Will you stay with me?"

"It will make parting more difficult," she said.

"Nevertheless, I heard a yes in there somewhere."

She smiled. "I can't justify giving up pleasure for the simple reason that it won't last. Nothing lasts forever."

"My feelings exactly. We have to live each day for the pleasure of itself. But one thing is changed. When you're in the castle, please don't wander off alone. You'll have to stay with me because I don't want you attacked like Pembroke and I were. It's the new rule of the castle lord."

"Something is going to have to be done about this dragon." Katherine sipped wine from a stemmed glass. "Reptile blood? How could it be?"

"More hoax, maybe. But would anyone anticipate we'd have the blood analyzed at a lab? One sure wouldn't think so."

"But if not, it means you have a large and vicious reptile residing in your gatehouse."

He shook his head. "I'd better design a dragon trap."

Katherine shuddered. "You're in danger. Those warnings were not gentle. Somebody wants you out of Aawn."

The waiter brought the chocolate cake that Mike had ordered, and coffee for her. He offered her half the cake, but she declined. He savored the first bite. "What could anyone gain by my leaving Aawn?"

"Maybe someone doesn't want the castle restored."

"If it isn't restored, it will fall into ruin like so many others. No, I can't believe that's the reason."

"Then someone wants a chance to buy it, like the former owners. Who are they?"

"A couple of businessmen who live in London. If they couldn't afford to keep it then, they certainly couldn't afford what I'd ask for it now, with the work that has been done. Damn, I just can't figure it."

"So why would anyone put the skeleton there? Maybe there really is a dragon. Did you ever think of that?"

He did not smile, nor meet her eyes. "Yes."

She studied him. "I thought so. There are so many unexplainable . . . things . . . in your castle."

"Well, we have to consider that the dragon might be getting blamed for stunts he isn't responsible for."

Katherine twisted the base of her glass and stared for a time at the flowers in the vase on their table.

"Let's get out of here," he said. "I want you in my bed again. I want to make love to you from now until morning."

Outside the restaurant she said, "If I'm going to stay with you, I'll need to pick up some things."

"Why not just check out?"

Her eyes met his. They were shining with passion and promise, and she had no power to resist them. Before she came to Wales he had told her they had no comfortable or proper accommodation for her. Proper was the operative word. Mike's huge bed by the fire was the most luxurious accommodation her creative imagination could ever have conjured up.

"All right," she agreed. "I'll tell Mrs. Mills I'm checking out. Can you deal with the gossip?"

"I couldn't care less about gossip."

She nodded knowingly. "As long as it is about you, you mean, and not about your resident dragon."

JUST BEFORE MIDNIGHT Katherine stirred in the bed, aware that Mike was not beside her. Because he had dozed after their lovemaking, she was surprised to find him gone so soon. She sat up, pulling the coverlet around her. Mike was sitting by the fire as she had done last night.... Was it only last night? The firelight shone softly, flickering on his naked body. He was a painting, an artist's masterpiece.

"I thought you were asleep," she said.

"I couldn't stay asleep."

"Neither can I. What are you thinking about?"

"You. About making love to you again. I can't get enough of you, my sweet."

"Then why didn't you stay and coax? You have marvelous and imaginative ways of getting my undivided attention."

"Umm. Watch out." He rose to set another log on the fire.

"What else were you thinking about? A dragon trap?"

"You know me pretty well."

"I know how angry you are. You aren't good at concealing anger. Today's attack on Pembroke was the last straw for you, wasn't it?"

"I'm not going to chance losing my dogs. I'm figuring a way of blocking off the dungeon area. I can't let go of the idea that the cave has an exit out of the castle. If I just knew how he's getting in, I'd have somewhere to start."

"He's clever. He'll expect you to try something."

Mike rose. He looked like a statue in the firelight. "Who wants to talk about it now? There are more important things on my mind. My dragon trap can wait till tomorrow." He kissed her and drew the cover away and propped thick, soft pillows beneath her head. "I want you, Kathy. Lie back and let me love you." He caressed her tenderly. His lips followed his hands, stroking, tickling, tasting.

She surrendered her body . . . her mind . . . her control, lost in passion mixed with trust. His lips, his breath, controlling her, using, giving, exquisitely torturing.

"Mike . . ." she breathed, her hands in his hair.

He whispered again, "Just let me love you. Let me take you to that special place . . . our special place. . . ."

She shivered into the final surrender, when her body tensed beyond endurance and turned to flame and then went limp and trembly, and she felt the warmth of his body rising over hers. And he took her away again, carrying her with him this time. His body was solid, forceful, fevered, overpowering. Conquering.

AFTERWARD SHE LAY in his arms. Strong young arms encircling her lovingly. Strong young arms to hold and protect her. Never before had Katherine been so aware of herself as a woman or wanted so deeply the love of a man. No man had ever given her so much. Or changed her so much. Katherine was aware of the changes taking place in her heart and her mind, but in the afterglow of his lovemaking, she had no inclination to try to define them.

"We have to live each day for the pleasure of itself," Mike had said. They had to, she agreed, because the alternative was scarcely to live at all. No tomorrows were ever guaranteed. The sadness in the joy of their love was the knowing it could not last. The sadness simultaneously weakened and strengthened the joy.

Now, in the dead of night, as she listened to his quiet breathing, the sadness was so overwhelming that she lay wondering if it might have been better had she never known....

No, it would not be better...no, it would not.

Sleep eluded her. She lay watching moving shadows of the flames on the wall as the fire burned down. It was easy to imagine that this very moment, down in the darkest bowels of the castle, a dragon was slinking. At the image, she cuddled closer to Mike, and he responded in his sleep by giving her a light, reassuring squeeze.

No, it was not imagination—that was the frightening part. The castle *was* haunted. The ghost of the dragon was here. Katherine knew it. And Mike knew it, too. He hadn't even tried to deny it.

No one would believe it, she thought. No one would believe any of this—*my knight of the castle, my knight of nights, making plans to slay a dragon* . . .

It would not be better to have never known him . . . or to have never loved him. She was changed forever, because of him. She was vibrantly alive. Never again would she run from a dream, if ever again, in her lifetime, she happened to find another.

10

PEMBROKE WAS ABLE to get up and down the stairs. She was no longer limping, but she was not yet ready for rabbit chases or rigorous outings. Sensing this, Talbot was willing to turn over the job of castle guard to Pembroke, while he trotted off behind Katherine toward the lakeshore.

Mike, having got nowhere with his trap plans, had gone off to work after breakfast, while Katherine sought solitude in the environs of the castle. Thomas, to her relief, had driven into the village for errands. This morning she wanted to be alone. The early clouds had been blown off by high winds. Now even the wind was calm and the water of the lake was still and the sun warmed her shoulders and sparkled on the water. Birds chirped and squawked in the trees.

She followed the erratic curves of the shore. The bracken was thick and green and wildflowers bloomed in profusion. The hills rolled down and spilled into the lake at the far edge. With the castle at her back, Katherine climbed the wooded slope. The hill crested sharply, then dropped rapidly again into a deep, bowl-shaped glen.

Breathing the wild beauty of the Welsh countryside, she hiked among the beeches and tall grass in the glen with the dog circling around and sniffing at logs and ground scents. He never strayed far, as if she were in his charge.

She sat down on a fallen log to rest. Talbot nestled up to her, wanting to be petted. Suddenly there was movement on the hillside, and a splash of red color against nature's green. A human figure appeared up there, as if by magic.

One moment the glen was deserted; the next, a figure was there as if it had dropped from the sky. The phenomenon was so strange that Katherine held the dog to silence and sat still, hidden in the shadows of the trees. She watched the human figure move down the hillside toward the floor of the glen and up again. He rounded the far crest and was gone.

In a few minutes Katherine heard a car engine start. She hadn't known there was a road beyond the bowl glen.

"How did a guy materialize out of air?" she asked Talbot. Excitement began to stir in her. She stood up, shading her eyes against the sun. "Unless he came out of the side of the hill!" Her heartbeat quickened. "Come on, Talb, old boy! Come on! We're going up there!"

Vegetation was thick, and so were the boulder-sized stones. Calculating the place where the man was standing when she first spotted him was difficult to narrow down because of that distance. She crossed over the area in wide circles. The dog sniffed out the scent of a human being, but even with his help the search proved futile.

Only after taking great care to study each landmark—the shapes of the bushes and rocks—did Katherine leave the hillside. She climbed back toward the top of the bowl. From its crest, she stood looking down on the back of the castle. A narrow stream wound its way across from the lake toward the western towers, where a moat had once been.

She ran down and crossed the stream by balancing on rocks that protruded from the water. The dog followed, leaping easily from one dry rock to the next.

Pembroke came out to meet them, tail wagging, as if to say, "Why were you two gone so long?" She seemed to have forgotten her injury, and was eager to romp with Talbot when they reached the inner court.

There were workmen in the bailey, loading lumber onto the lift. Mike was among them. Katherine had to wait until the load was being lifted by pulley to the windows of the Great Hall before she could talk to him.

"How was your walk?" he asked.

"Take a work break, Mike. I have something to tell you."

They sat on a stone bench in the glare of the midday sun. Mike wiped perspiration from his forehead.

"I'm not certain," she said, "but I think you're right about a cave exit. I might have discovered where it is."

His eyes flashed disbelief. "Are you serious?"

"Absolutely. I think a cave passage must extend under the first north hill, and come out on the slope just above that funny little valley."

She had his full attention. He straightened and sat tensely. "You found a cave up there? How is that possible, Kathy? I've been on that slope a hundred times."

"No, I didn't find a cave. I looked and I couldn't. But when I was down below, sitting with Talbot in the small grove, suddenly a person was standing on the hill. He didn't come down from the top nor did he climb up from the bottom. I'm sure, because I'd been looking. He just was suddenly there, like magic, on the hillside. The only possible explanation is that he came up out of the ground."

"Maybe the sun was in your eyes, honey. That's a fairly steep slope."

"I know what I saw. The person was wearing jeans and a red shirt. He walked down to the bottom of the glen and up the other side, and then I heard a car engine start up. I couldn't see him closely, but he had no hiking gear so he wasn't out for a hike. A car engine sounded from just over the hill to the northwest. Is there a road out there?"

"Not really. There are small trails here and there in the hills." He scratched his head. "Surely if there was an opening to the castle's cave, we'd have been told. Somebody would know about it."

"It appears as if someone does."

"But I'd have heard about it. People in the Llanhafod valley would know. It's almost two blocks between here and the place you describe."

"It isn't unusual for caves, or at least veins of caves, to be as extensive as that, and you know it."

"Yeah, but still . . ." He took her hand, and his voice grew softer. "Kathy, if you are right about this, it would explain a hell of a lot."

"Only if we can find the cave. The vegetation is thick on that hillside, but I have the location pinpointed." She studied him closely. "You don't believe me, do you?"

"It's just unlikely there's a cave nobody knows about."

"Are you going to help me look, or not?"

"Of course I am! Let's go."

Heading across a grassy slope toward the stream, Mike asked, "Are you sure you weren't seen by this guy on the hill?"

"Quite sure. I was hidden by the trees."

He circled his arm around her waist. "If you are right, this is an incredible stroke of luck."

Katherine could scarcely keep up with him. Talbot followed on their heels until they reached the stream, and then he ran ahead, toward the top of the hill.

"All these rocks and bushes," Mike said. "This will be impossible unless your calculations are accurate."

They searched for an hour without success. Finally, Katherine sat down on a rock to rest. In another ten minutes Mike joined her, plopping onto the ground near her feet. Talbot was upon him immediately, wanting attention.

"I'm beginning not to trust my own eyes," she said.

Leaning elbows against his knees, Mike answered, "If a connecting entrance to the castle cave was easy to find, it's existence would be common knowledge."

They sat in silence under a bright, still sky. Scarcely a breath of wind was blowing. The dog was panting and birds were singing and insects buzzed. Katherine laid her hand on his shoulder and closed her eyes. After a time, in the silence, she felt him straighten suddenly.

"Look at the leaves on those weeds over there, Kathy."

She opened her eyes.

He was pointing to the left. "Nothing else is moving, not a blade of grass, but those few leaves are blowing!"

Both leaped to their feet. Mike investigated the area of the blowing leaves, feeling the ground around a large boulder. Katherine watched, her heart quickening.

"There are strange, small gusts of wind . . . it has to be . . ." he was muttering, and his words were cut off by a grunt as he pushed aside the rock under which the draft seemed to originate. The boulder gave under his weight more easily than he anticipated. The stone rolled off a grassy cavern about three feet in diameter.

"I'll be damned!" Mike said.

"Good heavens!" Katherine exclaimed. "It is here! Oh, but look how small the opening is! A man couldn't squeeze in!"

"I couldn't, that's for sure. Your guy must have been pretty small."

"I couldn't tell. The hole would have been left open while he was inside. He couldn't roll it off from underneath."

Kneeling, Mike peered inside.

"Can you see anything?" she asked, bending close to him.

"No, it's too dark, but it has to extend because there is air coming up. Actually, Kathy, there are small caves all over this area and most have been blocked shut for decades because of the danger to livestock. No one who found this small hole would imagine it was the entrance to a long underground passage."

Kathy looked toward the hill that rose between them and the castle and shuddered. "How eerie to think this cave must go all the way through!"

"It must, though. Nobody would crawl in here without knowing what it is. Caves are too dangerous." He got to his feet and hugged her. "You're a gem, my love! This is how our dragon impersonator gets into the castle. We've got him! This is all the trap we need."

"You mean to block the cave after he's gone in, so his only way out is through the ward." She kissed his cheek. "If that works, it means you won't have to plot an encounter in the dark with some maniac wielding a knife!"

"We'll organize a simple operation. One person planted on the crest of the hill to watch for anybody coming in. A signal down to the castle, so we'll know the 'dragon' is in residence. And somebody to block this exit. Then all we'll have to do is wait. Damn, what a stroke of luck! I knew you'd be lucky for me. Knew it the first moment I saw you."

"Sure you did." Katherine smiled. "This plan sounds almost too simple."

"The best traps usually are."

Mike pushed the boulder back over the hole. "Our monster is not very big if he can get through here. I'm trying to think of any small guys who live in the village. There are several, but none I'd ever suspect of haunting my castle."

"There's a good chance he intends to come tonight," Katherine suggested. "If he was in the cave this afternoon, it could mean he's planning to come back."

"You mean, maybe he brought in sulphur bombs."

"I don't know why else he'd be hanging around, do you?"

Mike smiled wickedly. "We've got him now. Let's go back. We'll put our plan into action. First things first, though. All of a sudden I'm ravenously hungry."

He took her hand and they started up the slope.

"You're going to need some help with this," she said. "You can't be two or three places at once. And what exactly do you think will happen when the culprit materializes out of the gatehouse? Not a battle, I trust. Crimes have been committed here. I don't think you should try to handle the guy all on your own. It's what police are for."

"Spoilsport," he said lightly.

"It's no joking matter."

"You want to cheat me out of the pleasure of revenge? I want this character all to myself for just five minutes."

"Mike, be serious. This is going to result in scandal no matter how you handle it, so please be sensible and don't take unnecessary chances of getting hurt. You're going to have to enlist the proper authorities and break your silence about what's been going on in the castle."

"Yeah, I know it. I'll succumb to your superior common sense," Mike conceded, squeezing her hand affectionately. "I guess it's time to have a chat with the Llanhafod police."

They had reached the crest of the hill. He muttered, "It wouldn't be a challenge, anyhow, to take on a guy who's small enough to get through that little hole."

IN LATE AFTERNOON Katherine had been stationed as "watcher-on-the-hill" for an hour when Mike returned from the village and joined her there. He climbed up the slope behind the castle, without the dogs, who had been confined to the keep apartments, and sat down beside her in the shadows of a spreading rowan.

"Talking to the police was great fun," he said sourly. "If our prankster doesn't show up tonight, they'll probably lock me up in the nearest mental hospital."

Katherine looked at him. His eyes were not as worried as his voice. "They didn't believe you? But are they going to help?"

"They've sent two men out. As soon as we see anybody enter the hole, you can go down to alert the police while I block the entrance with a boulder. It might be a long wait, but with the only other exits blocked, sooner or later the guy has got to come out of the gatehouse into the ward."

Katherine grimaced at the thought of the dungeons of death. "The only thing that elevates this situation above a stupid game is the fact that you and Pembroke are injured, and someone could be again, unless this maniac is stopped."

"He will be." Mike circled his arm around her. "So. Are you having fun on your vacation, my dear?"

"Right now I'm not having as much fun as you are. Wouldn't it be ironic if that cave didn't go through, if it went somewhere else?"

He grinned. "No chance. This cave entrance provides an explanation for everything I couldn't figure out."

"Except a motive. And your imaginative hoax."

"I think we're soon to learn the motive." He repeatedly slapped fist against palm. "I hate waiting. I don't do it well. Distract me. Talk to me, Kathy. Tell me more about you. I know hardly anything about you."

"After four years of letters?"

"I've been reading over your letters. In summers they were scarce, and when they did come you said you were traveling. Normally people would describe their travels, but you never did, except maybe to make a comment about a certain town or the rainy weather. Why did you never write about your summer vacations?"

Katherine's eyes had become accustomed to the gray twilight as the afternoon turned to dusk. Mike was sitting close to her, his thigh and shoulder against hers. "It might sound silly to you, but I always thought of my summers as secret, known to no one but me. Guarding the secret became a habit, I think. I'd done it for so long it just never occurred to me to share it."

"Not even with—" He hesitated. "Someone so far away?"

"It wasn't the distance. It was you. I had a rather distorted impression of you then. I sensed you relating to my studious life-style and saw no purpose in disillusioning you." She paused. "That's not exactly the right word. What I mean is, I didn't want to shock you."

Mike shifted. "Shock me, Kathy, I beg you."

"All right, since you insist. For the past twelve years I've traveled with a circus on its summer circuit."

Mike absorbed her words. "I doubted you could shock me, but you've shocked me. Are you sure you're not making this up just to entertain me?"

She laughed. "The circus was owned by a family I have known since college. It closed for good at the end of last season because of financial hardships, so my circus days are over. Rather, I thought they were, until I came here."

"From the frying pan, as they say. I've got to hear about this! Did you perform?"

"Oh, sure. We all did. Mostly I worked with the animals, the elephants and horses and dogs. Or I filled in as clown."

"I'd kill to see it."

"What? The clown? You'd never recognize me."

"Not just the clown. All of it."

"I never thought I'd say this, but I almost wish you could have been there just once. I'd get a kick out of smiling at you from the center ring."

"I don't believe this," he said.

"Of course you do."

"Yeah, I do."

He touched her face. The lavender hills lay in silence. A crow cawed near the lake. Night seemed more eager than usual to descend from the tops of the farthest peaks. Katherine moved her hand over his.

Mike smiled. "You confessed your guarded secret to me."

"That's because now that I know you, I predicted your reaction. To some a circus is the end of the world. To you it would be a challenge. You see life as a challenge. Not only that, you've drawn out the less conventional side of me."

"In more ways than one." His eyes set on the grassy, rock-hewn ledge where anyone entering the glen would pop first into view.

"I remember going to a circus when I was a kid," he mused. "It was the first time I ever saw elephants, and there were beautiful women in skimpy costumes riding on their heads, waving. I was awestruck. Now, by damn, I'm picturing one of those women as you! Did you ride the elephants?"

"Oh, yes." She laughed. "I doubt there's another sensation like sitting on an elephant's head. It's like being lifted into a great gray sky and rolling with thunderclouds. Some day I want to find out where my elephant buddies are now, and go see them. They'll remember me, of course, being elephants. They always remembered, from summer to summer. We had wonderful reunions and sad farewells." Her voice dropped to a whisper. "The story of my life. Sometimes it seems as if all the joy life doles out is balanced by its weight in sadness."

"Yeah, it does seem that way," he agreed. "You are a remarkable woman. I knew it the first minute I saw you."

Katherine laughed. "I'm losing count of all the revelations since the first moment you saw me."

"I'll never forget that as long as I live. It's the most memorable moment of my life."

She said, "The moment was unforgettable for me, too."

He squeezed her hand. A cool breeze had blown up to chill the night air. Above, a few patches of white were showing through the low, dark clouds in the northwest sky.

He suddenly touched her arm. His body tensed. "They're here, Kathy!"

Three figures appeared over the shallow rim at the top of the valley. Dressed in dark clothes, they made their way down the slope, as surefooted as mountain sheep.

"Three!" Katherine whispered, leaning close. "What if one intends to wait here as a watch?"

"Then I'll have to incapacitate him. Hell, don't look so horrified. I didn't say kill."

"Just...be careful...." Her whisper was taken away by a tiny whiff of breeze that blew through the long grass.

In silence they watched the three circle down the narrow glen and back up the hillside until they stopped, shoved aside the boulder over the cave entrance, and disappeared as if swallowed by the low-crouching shadows.

Mike stood and offered his hand to Katherine. "It might be a long night before they decide to come out and face me," he said. "I'll see you back at the castle."

Katherine watched him make his way through the shadows toward the spot where three dark silhouettes had just disappeared. The twilight seemed suddenly colder as it settled around her.

Mike was in silhouette now, against the steel-gray sky. He was rolling a large boulder with his shoulders to cover the cave. A larger and heavier one than the boulder the three intruders had moved out of their way. For a moment longer Kathy watched him, marveling at the mystery of his strength. The excitement of the moment caught her up, and she turned and half ran down the slope toward the castle.

A police car was parked in the inner ward. Two men in uniform stood near the gatehouse smoking and talking. When they saw her hurrying in through the far curtained walls, both turned and walked in her direction.

"Three men entered the cave a few minutes ago," she told them, breathing hard from the rush down the hill. "Mike is blocking the cave." Earlier he had boarded shut the low entry into a passage that led from the lower floor of the gatehouse to a castle wing that connected with the ruins of the west tower. This isolated the tower completely. "He'll be back in a few minutes," she assured the young officers.

"We've but to wait, then," said the taller man. "You should take yourself to safety, lass."

The night, with stormy clouds, was closing in faster than it should have. Feeling a raindrop on her nose, Katherine looked up toward the darkening sky. Three or four birds that swerved and fell like bats in flight were circling over the ramparts of the massive tower. As she stood looking up at the sky and the darting birds, Katherine's eye caught a slash of red flame in one of the tower's high window slits.

Startled, she held her breath. The red spark was gone. The arrow slit where it had appeared was black. It could not have been a flashlight, because the light had been red as fire. Like a match with a red flame. Considering the distance from the hillside to the castle and the long, precarious, winding passage through the castle's bowels, it was impossible any of those men could have gone that distance that fast. And it wasn't likely that they'd head for the crown of the tower. Mike had told her no dragon "activity" had ever taken place up that high.

But something was up there.

Excitement pounding in her chest, she recalled the legends. In an ancient verse it was written that the glow from the beast's fire-breathing nostrils was sometimes seen for miles over the countryside, glowing in the tower slits as the monster went slinking along the twisting stairs at night.

Whatever it was, she knew this was the castle's ancient secret—something she would not have seen unless she was supposed to see it. Magic worked like that. And because of the magic, she was not afraid.

The three men who were at this moment crawling through the cold, twisting cave might harm her, as they had harmed Mike. The ghost of the dragon would not.

Mike had suggested she go up to the keep apartments with Thomas tonight. Katherine had resented this. Somehow she couldn't take the danger of the three pranksters seriously. Once they were out of their cover of darkness and in the spotlights on the bailey lawn, they might fight to avoid capture. But they were not going to fight her. Or the weapons of the police. She wanted to stay, to be witness to this wild adventure.

Her curiosity over the red glow was more powerful than any sense of obligation for pleasing Mike's overprotective whims. She had been moving slowly away from the two policemen, who were not on alert because it was too soon. Any moment now Mike would be back in the confines of the castle walls, and there would be no arguing with him over where he thought she belonged during the danger.

Unseen, she slipped into the shadows of the great tower and into its forbidding arches of stone.

There was no sound in the gatehouse. Below, beyond the horrid dungeon, three men were squirming and climbing like reptiles toward the castle itself. Had ancient enemies entered this way? Even if they had, they would not likely have ventured to the upper chambers, where they could be so easily cut off on the narrow, walled stairs.

Katherine hesitated only momentarily before she grabbed one of the flashlights that were kept in the foyer and turned onto the stairway. It was a familiar climb by now. With pounding heart but steady legs, she made her way slowly up the steep passage—drawn there by a force far stronger than fear.

Wind moaned through the window slits with mournful wails. Katherine groped at the walls, steadying her balance. A smell of sulphur wafted down so faintly that she was unsure whether it was real or imagined. Then came the clicking, the legendary clicking of giant claws against the stone, so soft at first she could barely hear it. The clicking got louder as she moved upward, propelled by curiosity so strong she couldn't have turned back if she'd tried. Curiosity surpassing any force that had ever driven her.

The stairwell widened at a landing, possibly the landing from where the flicker of red light blinked. Suddenly the sound of the wind changed. It was not the moaning wind she heard, but raspy, uneven sighs of heavy breathing. The cold tower became flushed with a rush of heat. Katherine stopped dead still as an enormous shadow moved behind her. Trembling with excitement mixed with terror, she shone the flashlight along the wall. The shadow was hovering there—a shadow of a giant, winged creature! Afraid to breathe, Katherine stiffened and forced herself to turn around.

She gasped and nearly lost her balance. Staring down through sparkling crystal eyes was the deathless dragon of Aawn.

11

THE MONSTER'S HEAD ROSE at least nine feet above the floor. Its scales shone iridescent green, crimson and lavender in the beam of Katherine's flashlight. The mouth was closed and the unblinking eyes shone like gemstones caught in moonlight. Gaping in disbelief, Katherine found herself frozen to the floor and mesmerized by the expression of the dragon's face. No viciousness was there, rather a regal kind of wisdom. Except for dilating nostrils, which were black, and except for a shuddering of the gold-tipped wings, the huge figure stood quite still, almost as if it did not want to frighten her by a quick movement.

Was it a ghost or was it real? Katherine extended an arm toward the dragon. Strangely, in the cold stone tower, a warmth emanated from the monster; she could feel it on her palm. How could warmth come from an apparition? But warmth or not, live eyes or not, it had to be only a ghost.

The huge three-toed claws clicked against the stone as the creature began to back into the shadows, and as suddenly as it had appeared, it was gone.

Katherine stood numbly, staring into a black void in the center of which a gold glow was slowly fading. She felt no fear, only awe and a tingle of excitement like standing in a rain of ice on a sweltering day. *There really was a dragon in Michael's castle!*

Would Mike believe this? Or did he already know?

Although the beast was no longer in sight, Katherine still felt its presence. Scarcely realizing where she was going or why, she made her way up the remaining flight of stairs toward the ramparts, and stepped out onto the parapet into the crisp night air. A cold moon had risen in the eastern sky. The countryside was bathed in gray light; the midnight-blue water of the lake was shot through with silver ripples. Standing with her back against the stone wall, Katherine remained so stunned by the appearance of the dragon that she had forgotten what was happening below.

When at last she did remember, she brushed cobwebs of mist from her eyes. How long she had stood there she had no idea. All she knew was she had needed that time alone to try to come to terms with the incredible thing she had seen. Now, starting down the steps, shining the light before her, she felt a sense of calm.

The tower was silent, but not empty. Somewhere in the darkness was the dragon.

Near the final steps came shouts, heavy footsteps and breaths like groans. A chase. Either Mike or one of the police officers was chasing someone, and they were on the stairs. Grinding her jaw against the cold rush of fear, she rounded the steps just as a figure of a man appeared, tearing up the steps of the gatehouse.

She raised the flashlight and shone it directly into his eyes, startling the man so thoroughly that he fell back in terror and would have landed on his head if Mike, directly behind, had not caught him and broken his fall. One of the policemen was behind Mike, ready with handcuffs.

Mike threw off the weight of the man, who was scarcely half his size, and looked up at Katherine with shock. "Kathy! You've been in the gatehouse?"

She stared down at him. "I've been...in the tower...."

He couldn't take his gaze from her while the officer was leading the captive away. To her surprise, he hadn't even bothered to confirm the identify of the prisoner.

"I'd have had a hell of a chase on my hands if you hadn't stopped that guy! How did you think that fast?"

She smiled, standing several steps above him. "Experience. Once a circus bear went on the rampage and came at one of the trainers. He used a flashlight to blind the bear long enough to get out of its way. When I heard the running footsteps, I remembered that incident, probably because I was holding a flashlight." She came down five steps to reach him. "Who are they, Mike? Did you catch the others?"

"They're kids!" he said incredulously. "The other two are girls! Can you believe that?"

"But that's bizarre!"

"Girls would be the logical choice, since most boys are too big to fit through the entrance passage. Except for this little twerp who tried to run. I recognize him as one of the kids from the village."

She frowned. "Logical choice? For what?"

"They were hired," Mike said. His hand circled her waist and he guided her into the gray night. Ahead of them the policemen were leading the three captives to the car. Katherine looked at Mike, whose hair was blowing in the breeze. His broad shoulders formed a hulking shadow in the moonlight.

"They were hired by whom?"

He shrugged. "They realized how much trouble they were in, and were afraid to talk."

"You must have some idea."

"All I can do is look to my enemies. I've made a few enemies, both in my personal life and in business, but it's hard to think of anyone going to this kind of trouble to get back at me."

"What enemies might have some knowledge of the castle?"

He scratched his chin. "Information can be bought as easily as local kids can be bought."

Katherine gazed at him, wondering what in his past might trigger enough hatred to spawn a scheme as crazy as this. "It couldn't be an environmental group who is bitter over your selling your car design to the oil companies, could it?"

"Who could be that stupid? The car wouldn't have been manufactured whether I sold out or not. There were too many people between me and the finished product. We're grasping at straws, Kathy."

"What else is there to grasp at? But surely the teenagers will talk to the police to avoid taking full blame."

"We'll see. I don't think these kids were capable of planting that fossil. It was too expertly done. My feeling is that the hoax has been there for some time. It might not have anything to do with them."

She looked at him. "You do have an idea, don't you?"

"Not really. I'm just trying to cover all bases."

"Tell me."

He ran his fingers through his hair. They were walking through the bailey. By now the lights of the police van were shining along the still, dark ribbon of road. The police had been in a hurry to leave, preferring to interrogate the teenagers at the station.

"Tell me the straw you're grasping at," she repeated.

He shrugged. "It's crazy, but then so is everything else around here. I was thinking about . . . my ex-wife. According to what I've been told, she has lost a lot of money in the last year. Lost isn't the best word—she was conned out of it by a man who pretended to be a rich bachelor in love with her. He was neither rich nor a bachelor. She also resents the hell out of my owning a castle." He smiled at the woman who was walking beside him in the Welsh night. "People think of castles as massive, luxurious mansions, don't they? My attorney tells me she is trying to find ways of getting more money out of me, that she's desperate to do so. She's the only person I can think of who might think she'd benefit if I were driven to sell this monstrosity." He turned. "Kathy, why are you looking at me like that? It's only a farfetched theory."

She stared, feeling his words like blows of stone. "Ex-wife? Mike, you said your wife was dead!"

He winced. "I never said that...."

"You did! You wrote it to me. And you talked about it."

He hesitated. "You misinterpreted some of that."

She wished it were possible to see his eyes in the dark. "Did I? Which part?"

Mike cleared his throat. "It was a bitter divorce. I think of that whole part of my life as dead. I don't know what was in the letter, but I didn't deliberately lie about it. I'm sorry. I shouldn't have even brought it up." He combed through his hair again with his fingers. "She's damned creative about money. I just can't think of anyone else with enough motive."

Katherine saw him in a new, hard light. Had Mike believed Katherine of Allendale would think less of him if she knew about his bitter divorce? Perhaps. He'd thought her very sheltered. Still, she was sure of what he'd written. Were there other lies, too?

He had stopped walking. In the cold moonlight he turned to her. "We'll—we'll talk about this if you want."

"What else don't I know about you?"

He frowned. "You know my life, Kathy. College, a corporate job, a marriage that went sour, my bailing out of the whole scene and coming here. That's it."

She tried to smile, remembering how much of her life she had kept from him. He didn't, after all, *owe* her anything. "I'm not judging you, Mike. Perhaps I did misunderstand...."

"It isn't important now," he answered, taking her hand. "Tell me what happened in the tower. I saw the look in your eyes. What have you been wanting to tell me?"

Her heart beat stronger. She leaned close for support. "Mike, do you know what really is in the tower?"

He looked at her, half frowning, half smiling, hesitating.

Her excitement and impatience exploded. "Well! Do you?"

"Yes."

Her thumping heart leaped to her throat. "My God, Mike!"

His voice shook. "You saw it?"

"Yes. I saw the dragon."

Mike fell into a strange silence. Neither noticed the rain or the mud forming in the path. They ought to be screaming, she thought. A thing as unbelievable—as impossible—as this ought to have them howling. Instead, Mike retreated into silence, and she still felt the unusual calm she had experienced in the castle. Mike, obviously, felt it too. How odd that the discovery of a thing could bring this peace in its wake.

Finally she asked, "Why didn't you tell me it was there?"

"I did tell you."

"You made it sound like . . . a ghost!"

"It is a ghost."

"Is it? Mike, if you had seen a thing like that, at least you might have—"

"No one else has seen it," he interrupted. "I had no way of knowing you would ever see it. I preferred that you not think I'm crazy."

She chewed her lip. "How often have you seen it?"

"Only once. Only that night I found the bones. I had felt its presence often. But it's been only since you came that the thing showed itself to me. It wasn't just the skeleton that kept me in the gatehouse all through that night."

They ducked into the entry. "Did it frighten you?"

"At first, hell, yes," he answered. "But once I got a look at the face, I knew it wasn't vicious. The face was almost . . . friendly . . . stupid as that sounds."

"It was regal and wise," she said. "I wasn't afraid of it, either, after the first horrendous shock."

Mike moved his hand along the back of her neck. "That's a relief. The dragon traditionally doesn't like women. He lures them into complacency and then eats them for a snack."

"The legend is obsolete, then! I have no fear of being eaten." She paused. "Nor will I tell anybody what I saw."

"Good. I hoped you wouldn't, for all our sakes. It's unbelievable enough at Aawn. Back in your town of Allendale, I don't think they would understand. It'll be our secret." He touched her cheek gently. "Someday, Kathy, when you are far away from here, you will look back on this summer and think you only dreamed it. And maybe I will, too."

His words caused tears to form behind her eyes. "Do you think he'll show himself again?"

"I don't know. I have a feeling that when you're gone, he won't."

WITH NO NEWS WHATSOEVER from the police Mike took the rest of the week off to show Katherine his adopted country on her last few days of vacation. They toured mountain forests, old market towns and the enormous castles of King Edward I. They visited busy summer seaside resorts, drove through the once-dark landscapes of coal-mining country—landscapes that were greening once again now that the mines were shut down. They walked the free, wild beaches of the Gower Peninsula where the green pastures rolled down into white sands washed by tides.

In those days of touring, she came to understand Mike better, came to understand what she already knew—that he was so involved in the monumental task of restoring a castle that he had made no provision in his life for a woman. He had been burned badly; his suspicion of his ex-wife proved how much. He cared for Katherine, this too was plain. But he thought of her as a summer romance, as if he, through no planning of his own, had found himself caught up in a dream that belonged to her.

So it was a summer dream, nothing more. Summer magic, spawning sunlit love. Summers did not last forever.

When they returned to Aawn again, the sinister old castle felt like home to Katherine. Its long murky passages, its creaks and groans were as familiar as the squeak of a screen door and songs of crickets in summer grass at home. Aawn had become part of her forever. Perhaps no one but Mike could understand. He was as much a part of this old fortress as those who lived before him in its medieval halls. The ancients defended Aawn; Mike was restoring it. Perhaps only those who resided here ever knew the castle's awesome secret. Except for her.

Thomas had news when they returned. He led them up to the privacy of the keep apartment and sat them down with a glass of sherry, and said, "While you were away the police found out who hired your three dragonettes. The man's name is Henry Boyle. He's a business partner of the former owners of Aawn. Londoners, all of them."

Mike sat back and watched his father take his time lighting his pipe, as if he knew it would do no good to hurry him. Katherine, on the edge of her chair, felt a flood of relief that this had nothing to do with Mike's former life.

"They had a good sum invested in this castle," Thomas continued finally, puffing as he talked. "They were trying to raise more funds when it was sold out from under them. This Boyle evidently has just joined the other two, and he seems to be the perpetrator of the violence. The girls have come forth with the agreement and the payments. The boy, who I understand is the village troublemaker, has admitted to attacking you and the dog, trying to say it was unintentional. Even the reptile blood was part of the scheme. What the kids were originally hired to do was scare you off. When that didn't work, they were asked to find a way to get the hoax out of the castle before it was discovered. The dragon legends were the main lure of this castle, that's why they created the hoax. After all the money they had sunk into that fake fossil, they wanted it back to try to use in another location."

Mike leaned forward to refill his drink. "What kind of idiots would spend fifty thousand pounds on a stupid dragon hoax when they didn't have enough to meet the mortgage payments?"

Thomas laughed. "That is precisely what I asked. From what I have been able to learn, they didn't anticipate financial trouble. A third investor backed out. The hoax was supposed to bring so much publicity the money would start rolling in. The guys are all in the field of advertising—it's their mind-set. They were more interested in bringing attention to the place than in getting the renovation done."

"And they probably underestimated the cost of renovation," Mike surmised. "Like we all did."

"No doubt. In any case, they wanted the dragon bones back since we weren't being scared off by the attacks." Thomas puffed diligently on his pipe. "Of course, if we had been scared away, the publicity generated by that would have added to the intrigue of the place. It was all carefully planned."

"It was stupid as hell," Mike grumbled. "These idiots have no more business sense than common sense. Have charges been officially made against them?"

"Yes, and the kids are cooperating."

Mike's shoulders sagged in relief. He turned. "You're awfully quiet over there, Kathy. What are you thinking about?"

"The dragon," she answered softly, her eyes shining. "The stories of the dragon getting rid of those he doesn't want in his domain. These men don't know how lucky they are that their scheme didn't work. They don't belong here."

Mike gazed at her intently. Kathy had changed since she'd seen the dragon, just as he had. She talked of the castle as though it were a living thing. She, too, had found its soul.

After Thomas had finished his tale, Katherine and Mike walked hand in hand through the blue shadows of summer twilight. Pembroke and Talbot romped around them, chasing the scents of rabbits and squirrels. A crescent moon was hanging over the distant hills. In the stillness, they could hear the gurgling of the nearby stream. The song of the stream was different at night. To this they had both agreed, but they had never determined why.

She had become used to the night song of the stream, and to the sparkle of morning sun on the water. She was used to the sweet scent of the wood-burning fires, and to the crisp early-morning chill. She was used to the echoes in stone hallways, and to the wind whipping through arrowloops on the tower stairs. And she was used to Mike beside her in the night, used to his breathing and to the warmth of his touch. Katherine felt more at home here than she had ever felt in Allendale. It had to do with belonging. Of being part of a world that most people could never understand.

Tomorrow it would be over.

In the west the blue twilight was tinted with splashes of pink and gold. Walking back toward the castle from the lakeshore, Katherine asked, "Will there be a trial?"

"I suppose so," he answered. "I don't care much. As long as these guys are off my back, that's all that matters to me. I haven't got time for revenge. I just want to get on with my uncomplicated life."

"You're very good at closing chapters, aren't you?"

Mike tensed and squeezed her hand tightly. "Not always. I can do it if I have to, but that doesn't mean I'm good at it." He frowned. "I wish circumstances were different . . . with us, I mean. I wish I . . . had something to offer. I haven't, though. I haven't anything but this old ruin."

Katherine wondered if he was trying to spare her feelings or make her feel worse. He had made it clear from the start that their togetherness was only temporary. She had felt the same, at first. She had felt that way because of his age. Now she thought of their age difference only as something for other people to remark about.

And Mike? Did their age difference matter to him in the long run? He was obviously incapable of thinking of them being together after this summer. Whether it was her age or his obsession with his work, or whether he simply did not care for her enough, he would not ask her to stay.

Katherine's eyes were on the sky, where the last rays of daylight were turning from pink to gray. A night-hunting hawk circled down from the hills. From along the water's edge came a chorus of fluting frog's songs, welcoming darkness.

Above the courtyard stars were blinking silver and gold against a velvet cover of midnight blue. Katherine imagined Mike's ancestors looking up at just such a sky on just such a summer night.

It was a different world now, a world where people in love could not always share their dreams. She was trying hard not to show Mike the awful unease wrenching her heart. She could not stay.

Even Aawn did not exude enough magic to make Mike love her enough. This had been a dream in midsummer in a magic castle. Never quite real. Not real enough to last.

She lay in his arms that last night with the fireplace coals glowing and the hanging bed rocking like a cradle on its heavy chains.

"The next tomorrow will be longer than forever," she said.

"I'll miss you, too. More than I can say." Mike touched her cheek. "Maybe you'll come back someday."

"Yes . . . maybe."

He snuggled next to her, breathing on her neck. His naked body felt both cool and warm against her. His hands caressed her throat and her breasts. He kissed her deeply.

"Kathy...just one more time let's pretend there is no tomorrow. There is only tonight. Kiss me...make love to me...."

12

DAWN CAME in shades of moody gray. Even before she was fully awake, tears had formed in Katherine's eyes. She opened them to see, through the blur of tears, that Mike was awake and watching her.

He leaned over and kissed her eyes. "Don't cry, honey. I can't bear to see you cry."

"In that case, I'm not crying."

His fingertips caressed her cheek. "I wish you didn't have to go."

"But I do have to."

He stroked away a tearstain from her cheek. "Our time together is the happiest I've ever been, Kathy."

"Then it's good...our having met."

"Not all good. I'll be bitter when you're gone, though not entirely alone because your spirit will always be in this castle to remind me of the sweetest summer of my life."

The ache inside her was excruciating. "You're going to make me cry again and I want you to remember me laughing."

Why are we saying goodbye? her heart screamed.

But her mind knew why. They were two people from different worlds, opposite life-styles, different dreams.

Hell, she thought. *I would forfeit my life-style in a second. I'm going to leave Allendale for good next year. After this summer, Allendale will be too dull to bear.*

Was it valid to say she and Mike had different dreams? No. Their dreams were alike, but Katherine refused to allow herself to dwell on this thought. Mike's mind was made up. For him the summer and the love affair were over.

They didn't fit, the two of them. She, the thirtyish spinster of Allendale, and he, a young man pursued by every eligible female in town. It was too crazy to think about. Even now. A man like Mike wouldn't try to hold on to her.

But he held her tightly now, in the warmth of his bed. They lay in silence, each coiled in the sadness of private thoughts. The morning, while they were living it, was becoming memory already. "What time is it?" she asked.

"Half past eight."

"It's so late. I must get up and shower."

"What time are you due in the village to meet your coach?"

"I don't have to go into the village. I left word for the driver to pick me up at the crossroads. The coach will be here at nine-thirty."

"That's only an hour from now!"

"Don't I know!" Katherine drew back the fur cover, climbed out of bed and headed for the bathroom.

Before he dressed, Mike put a log on the fire so the room would be warmed for her.

On the level below, Thomas was waiting. "I've made breakfast," he said when they came in.

"Oh, Thomas, I haven't time! Oh, but thank you." She hugged him and kissed his cheek. "Thank you for everything."

His pale eyes were sad. "So now you return to your other world, and leave our poor old castle as empty as our hearts."

Katherine grasped Thomas's thin hands in her own.

"I have something for you," he said, and produced the book on Aawn's history that the three of them had pored over on cold nights by the fire. Mike had often quoted from the book in his letters to her.

"But that book belongs here at the castle, Thomas," she protested. "I couldn't—"

"I have managed to find another copy. A village called Hay-on-Wye, right on the English border, has more used books than any other place in the world, and a bookstore there has searched for and found another. They are delivering it out to me. So please take this one as a souvenir."

"Thank you," she said. "Nothing could I treasure more."

Mike stood in sullen silence. He picked up her bags and carried them down the steps, and loaded them into the back of the truck.

The dogs, sensing the goodbye, followed behind the truck down the tree-lined lane for a quarter mile until it came to a stop at the crossroads.

"This is hell," Mike said.

She merely nodded.

"Kathy..."

Fighting back tears, she looked over at him.

He stammered over his words, started and stopped and fidgeted. And finally said, "Be happy."

"You, too."

When they saw the coach approaching they got out and Mike lifted her bags from the back. Katherine petted each of the dogs.

She saw that there were tears in his eyes as he gathered her in his arms and kissed her. The day was dark gray; skies were spitting rain. Up on the bright green hillsides, sheep grazed peacefully. The castle loomed in the near distance, silent and ominous, guarding its secrets. The sound of the approaching engine seemed a thousand times louder than it really was. He held her tightly and when words wouldn't come, he kissed her again.

The coach drew to a stop a few feet away. Katherine felt stares from the other passengers, but nothing mattered at that moment except the hideous realization that she was never going to see Michael again.

The driver loaded in her bags and opened the door for her. She could no longer feel her feet under her.

The engine started and the coach lunged forward. Through a blur of tears, Katherine looked back as the vehicle rumbled down the road, carrying her to another world that was supposed to be her world. Mike, in the same tight jeans he had worn when she first saw him, was standing in the middle of the road, watching the vehicle disappear, the dogs standing motionless at his side—three silhouettes in the gray-white light of the drizzly morning.

MIKE TURNED AWAY after the coach had disappeared over the crest of a hill, and wiped his eyes with the sleeve of his sweater. His chest was heavy. Numbness weakened his limbs. He felt a severe headache coming on.

Thomas was expecting him for breakfast, but he couldn't face his father this morning. To put on a courageous front required too much self-control, and he couldn't bear the thought of having to talk about Katherine. Not yet.

He needed time.

Thomas, however, was impatient. Two hours after Mike had gone to work in the Great Hall, his father went looking for him.

Work was the only thing Mike knew to do with himself that morning. In spite of the headache, he tried to concentrate on the tasks at hand—tasks that brought him each hour closer to his dream of a castle inn. Katherine's absence, so deeply felt already, made the dream less easy to define.

Pulling up boards placed long ago over a portion of the stone floor, Mike didn't see his father approach.

Thomas laid a hand on his shoulder. "You've missed breakfast and lunch," he said.

Mike did not answer, but he stopped prying at a board that was giving him trouble.

"I've got coffee and some sandwiches made. Come upstairs. I want to talk to you."

"Can it wait, Dad?"

"No, it can't."

Mike acquiesced to Thomas's commanding voice and his own throbbing head. He pushed his hair away from his eyes and followed his father out of the hall.

Upstairs, he swallowed three aspirin. Thomas poured coffee at the dining table and waited for Mike to sit down. He did, in silence, and picked up the steaming coffee mug gratefully. At last Thomas said it—the question Mike knew was coming and dreaded.

"When is Katherine coming back to Aawn?"

He winced. "She isn't, as far as I know."

Thomas took a sip of the hot coffee. "So you let her go."

"I had no choice, Dad. Her vacation was up. She had to catch her flight home."

"Umm. So Katherine is on her way to the Manchester airport and you are sitting here in your tower looking more dead than alive."

"I've got a pounding headache."

"You're about to give me one." He shoved the plate of sandwiches to Mike, who shook his head. "I don't understand. No man of sound mind would let that woman get away."

"Dad, please. I'm in no mood to discuss it right now."

"We're going to discuss it anyway. I've watched the two of you. I've never seen two people more compatible in my life. Or any two who seemed happier together."

Mike held his head. "Have some mercy, will you?"

"I don't feel merciful, I feel brutal. I haven't felt this brutal in years. I want to know why you let her go."

"Because Katherine Glenn is out of my class."

"Class? You're Michael Thomas Reese, Junior! You have a claim to class! You've inherited class! Oh, well, granted, you're a little rough around the edges, but that's only your youth. I think your rough edge is what attracted Katherine."

"I don't want to talk about it."

"I wasn't aware of giving you a choice."

Mike raised his head and glared at his father. "Look, Kathy doesn't even know who I am, thanks to you. You and that stupid lie. I'd think you would be glad to have her gone before she found out that I'm not you. She still thinks I'm you."

"It's hard to imagine that she could. The differences in us—"

"She could, because it would never occur to her that we would lie to her, that's how! What do you suppose she'd think of me if she discovered I'm a fraud? She would have found out if she'd stayed here much longer. Eventually I wouldn't have been able to stand it anymore and would have told her. And hurt her. Hurt both of you."

"You're never going to make me believe that the reason you let her go is to protect our lie. I know you better than that. The kid I raised will stop at nothing to get what he wants—this castle project is proof enough of that. I'm trying to find out if I read you wrong, which I rarely do. I want to know if you allowed her to leave out of cowardice, stupidity, or because you don't want her."

Mike looked away. "You're talking like I had a choice. Kathy wouldn't stay here. She's a lady who deserves roses and champagne every day of her life. What have I got to offer her? A cold, drafty ruin in the middle of nowhere."

"So that's it." Thomas reached for his pipe.

"Yeah, that's basically it. A man has his pride."

His father puffed in the irritating way he always did when he was about to make a serious point that was meant to eliminate all competing points. "I suppose you think she'd be happiest with . . . say . . . a younger version of myself."

"Not for a minute. She'd be bored to death with a younger version of yourself."

"Of course she would. Katherine is too vibrant a woman to settle in for a lifetime with a tame and scholarly type—the sort who would naturally be most available to her. It's probably why she hasn't married. What she wants, dear boy, is not champagne and roses.

Katherine wants adventure and—first and foremost—a steely and virile man."

"How do you presume to know what Katherine wants?"

"That is precisely what you've been doing—presuming to know what she wants!"

Mike took a sip of the cooling coffee and set the mug down hard. "Steely and virile man, huh? I hope you are not referring to me as a point of reference. She came here thinking I was sick."

"Too bad she can't see how sick you look right now." Thomas blew smoke over the table. "Let's stop tiresomely skirting the issue. I've seen how the two of you were together. Are you in love with her?"

"That is not the issue."

"Of course it's the issue! If you love a woman, you don't let her walk out of your life. You ask her to stay in your life. Did you ask her to stay?"

"No, because I didn't want to put her in the uncomfortable position of turning me down. She wouldn't have a guy like me, and I'm getting sick of talking about it."

"How do you know if you don't ask?"

"Because she's too smart not to turn me down."

Thomas laughed without amusement. "Of course. Katherine is holding out for a routine life filled with material possessions. Ah, the good life! Routine schedules and VCRs and self-cleaning ovens. A new car in the garage. Membership in a health club and a country club. Bridge on Tuesdays, golf on Thursdays. Just what every woman wants, right?"

"Dad, stop it, please."

"All right, I'll stop. But I had to have my say. If you want to throw away Katherine's love, there's nothing I can do about it. Are you going to eat or not?"

"No. My headache is ten times worse than it was when I sat down here. I'm going upstairs and lie down."

HE COULD NOT LIE STILL. The bed smelled of Katherine's perfume. It was still warm from her body. When he closed his eyes she was still there, close, reaching to him.

The throbs in his head drummed the same words over and over. *I miss you, Kathy. Damn, I miss you.*

She had never said she loved him. But she had made love to him as no woman ever had. She had responded to his love as no woman ever had. The beating of her heart had said she loved him. Her eyes had said it.

He himself had never said those three words, either. He had been afraid, because it was understood from the beginning that whatever they had was temporary.

Wasn't it?

Moments they had shared flashed through his mind. He saw her eyes, her smile, heard her laughter. He felt the warmth of her hand in his as they strolled the lakeshore and rolled on the grass and ate in candlelight and lay together.

She's holding out for a life of routine and material possessions, his father had said with cold sarcasm. Good God! Not his Kathy. She wasn't his ex-wife. Any woman could have a life of creature comforts. Kathy put no value on those things. She was holding out for more . . . a lot more.

Kathy wanted challenge. She wanted magic. She had told him so herself! He had seen how the sight of the dragon had affected her. He had seen how she accepted what no one else could. The dragon—the monstrous ghost who walked in this castle—had shown itself to her. Only to Mike . . . and to her! What better proof could there be that she belonged here? Why the hell hadn't he let himself see it?

Mike shot into a sitting position. *Katherine had told him what she wanted, and he hadn't heard.*

Mike looked at his watch. Already after three. If he hurried, he might make Manchester airport before she left!

He changed into a wool sweater and pulled on clean jeans. Racing down the winding steps, he peered into the lower apartment only long enough to yell to his father, "If I can find somebody to fly me to Manchester, I can stop her before her plane leaves. It'll be close, but I think I can make it."

IT TOOK THIRTY MINUTES on the country roads to reach the local airstrip. No pilot was immediately available, so he had to wait, pacing, drinking coffee and cursing himself. By the time they were airborne, his pilot was confident they would reach Manchester just after six.

They did, but the small plane had to land on an airstrip a good distance away. By the time Mike had found a shuttle, reached the international terminal and checked the number of Katherine's flight, the gate doors were already closed and the plane was taxiing along the runway. Gasping for breath from running, Mike stood in the terminal with crowds at his back, watching the Boeing 747 circle into its takeoff position. Within moments it was in the air.

The crowd swallowed him. Airport noises slammed torturously at his brain. He had almost made it, but almost wasn't good enough.

Katherine was gone.

13

ROSALIND, WEARING WHITE linen slacks and a mint-green silk sash, waved excitedly and rushed up to give Katherine a hug. "Oh, Kath! How wonderful to have you back! And just in time for my garden party!"

Katherine returned her sister's loving squeeze. "Just in time? The party is two weeks away."

"We had to set up the date because of the mayor's schedule. It's next Saturday. I've only three days to get all the last-minute details together. You look tired, Kath! How was your adventure? You didn't write and tell me a blessed thing, and I lost sleep wondering. What was he like, your castle lord?"

"He was . . . a surprise." She fell into step with her sister as they walked to the luggage claim area. "How are Rusty and the kids? Is everyone fine?"

"Is that a deliberate change of subject? I want to know everything, even if it was less than what you expected. Those things usually are. Yes, everybody is fine. Rusty has spent the summer taking videos and lolling weekends away in the Jacuzzi. The girls are still at summer camp. Can we go to the house so I can show you my party dress?"

Katherine smiled. "Roz, have a heart. Look at these circles under my eyes. I'm exhausted. I'll be lucky if I get rested up in time for the blasted bash."

Rosalind gasped dramatically. "You are calling the Allendale social event of the year—my garden party—a blasted bash?"

"Forgive me," she said evenly. "I'm not myself. I'll see your dress tomorrow when I surface again. Right now all I can think about is a cup of tea and crashing into bed."

Rosalind pointed to the conveyor belt where her bags would come out. "Now tell me about this eccentric millionaire you were writing to. What is he like? Too terribly eccentric?"

"He's nothing in real life like he was in his letters, but he's . . . very nice. To tell you the truth, Rozzie, I'd just as soon discuss Michael Reese later, when we have time to sit down and chat. Right now you've got party arrangements on your mind, and my mind is so numb I'm barely functioning."

"Okay. Sounds as if you haven't a great deal to tell, anyhow. This Michael was obviously not what you'd expected." Rosalind adjusted her sash impatiently. "Oh, Kath, wait until you see the flowers I've ordered. And the ice sculptures, and eight crates of champagne. The party is costing Rusty a fortune, but he is the one who keeps insisting we must have only the best. You knew he's running for the state senate next year, didn't you? Two congressmen are coming Saturday, and all the women in town are talking about their gowns. I'm worried about what on earth you have to wear, Kath."

"I'll find something."

"You always say that," Roz said dejectedly.

"Don't worry about it," Katherine insisted. "I'll find . . . something."

Nothing will ever change in Allendale, she thought with a sinking heart. Every summer it was a shock coming back to values that were not her own, to a life-style that almost choked her after the summer's free-dom. It was no wonder she had always pulled away and lived her own life and been accused of not wanting to fit in. Each year, in the short interim between returning home and the start of the school year when she could immerse herself in work she loved, Katherine always asked herself the same question: Why the hell did she stay?

This summer, the first summer after her mother's death, she had asked herself the question a thousand times. For many years while Roz had been too busy, Katherine had been emotional support for her wid-owed mother. This summer she had been honest enough with herself to understand why she had stayed in Allendale—because she had never found a place she did belong. In the back of Katherine's mind, with all her summers of travel piling up, she had believed she would find home. The circus was the closest she had ever come.

Her mother had needed her in Allendale and her well-paying job was one she loved. It left her summers free and her winters filled with the joys of teaching history.

A restlessness was always there, in Allendale, but it followed her other places, too. She had never found what it was she was looking for. In the back of her mind she had always believed in magic.

And she had found it. The magic of Aawn would live in her forever. The lesson she had learned was that one can find magic but one cannot hold on to it.

Returning home this time, listening to Roz obsess about her garden party, Katherine felt the shock more than ever before. A party was the center of Allendale's universe. Although used to it, the shallowness of this mind-set had never depressed her more.

She woke to the brightness of an August day. Sun streamed in through the windows of her town house. The ache of missing Mike was unbearable. She saw him standing in the rain with the dogs at his side. It had been all she could do to stop herself from jumping out of the coach and running back into his arms . . . back into his world where she belonged. How could life change so completely and so quickly?

The phone rang. Roz already. Katherine glanced at the clock. A quarter past eight. She went into the bathroom and turned on the shower, and let the phone keep ringing.

Afterward, wrapped in a terry robe, her hair damp, she stood in front of a neat row of her best dresses hung in the guest-room closet, trying to decide. The exercise was a form of self-induced torture. One by one she pulled dresses from the closet, each with its own memories of her social life in Allendale. One by one she threw them on the floor with an angry flourish. "How could I have worn this stuff?" she asked aloud. "Who is the drab frump who picked this thing out? And this! Good lord, and this?"

Her Allendale clothes. Her Allendale identity. A lump formed in Katherine's throat. The woman who wore these frocks was almost a stranger to her. The Katherine of Allendale was a ghost. The Katherine of Allendale had never been completely real; this was painfully apparent now.

Mike had changed her.

Mike and his enchanted castle had made her see herself, not as the illusion she showed the world, but as the person she really was. Mike's loving had given her back her youth and the joy of being a woman. Even in the throes of heartbreak, she felt more vibrant, more alive than ever before. Because of him. Because of what they had shared.

Mike loved the gypsy in her. It was the gypsy the dragon came to—the Katherine who believed the magic. What an idiot she had been to try to hide her real self because she didn't know where the real Katherine belonged! All those summer secrets. What a coward she'd been!

It took a man with a heart as free as hers to make her understand and accept her secret heart. She had this, at least, from Michael. And the precious memories. Even though she had lost the man.

With her heart aching, Katherine tore every remaining dress from its hanger and threw it onto the heap on the floor. This time there was no going back to being the woman who wore those. No going back to the woman she was before Mike.

The phone rang again. She answered with a crisp hello.

"Kath, where were you? I rang earlier."

"In the shower."

"Are you coming by?"

"If you want me at the party, I'll have to go shopping. I'll be optimistic and presume there's something left in the Allendale shops after every woman in town has been shopping for this party."

"You didn't find anything suitable in your closet? Oh, thank goodness! You're so hopelessly conservative and this is most definitely not the occasion for conservative. Try Cecilia Stuart's boutique. She might have something."

"All right, I'll try Cecilia's."

"Good! I wish I could go with you, but the caterer is coming out, and anyway, every time we try shopping for clothes together, it leads to a fight." Roz droned on. "The decorations in the garden are absolutely stunning. I can't wait for you to see it. When this party is over, we must have that long talk. I want to hear all about your summer."

Katherine hung up with a sigh. She wasn't sure what she would tell Roz. Probably not the truth, because Roz would not believe a man like Mike could love her. Even for a summer.

Before she was ready to leave for the dreaded shopping spree, Katherine's doorbell rang. "Express delivery from England," the young man said when she opened the door. "There's no address number here, just a street name, but I knew where to find you."

Katherine's first thought was that it couldn't be from Mike. He knew her address, after all the letters he had written—but she hoped, anyway.

Inside the envelope was a single sheet of yellow paper, written in a heavy, scrawling hand. Katherine had read no more than a few words of this letter when she began to shake.

"Kathy, dear, I'll mail this express from the Manchester airport, so it will fly over right behind you. I rushed to try to catch you before you left and damn my luck, I missed your plane by minutes. I wanted to ask you to stay longer. We have some things to talk about." Here were scrawls and scratches where he had deleted an entire sentence. "Never mind right now," the letter continued. "I'll phone you. Love, Mike. P.S. I miss you like crazy."

Katherine stared at the page. *What was this?* This was not Mike's handwriting!

Horror swept over her. Katherine slumped onto a chair in her sun-filled living room and read through the mysterious letter again. Her heart pounded with a terrible foreboding. Her hands shook. Had Michael gone to Manchester to ask her not to leave so soon? Was that possible? And if he had gone all that way and missed her departure by minutes . . . and then hurriedly written . . . ? She gazed at the yellow paper. *Who wrote this letter?*

Who could have written this letter, if not him? No one!

Except Thomas? Thomas wouldn't sign Mike's name to a letter! Thomas wouldn't rush off to Manchester and then send a hurried note by express mail and claim that he was Mike.

Katherine jumped to her feet. Thomas's handwriting was in the book he gave her the morning she left Aawn. She made a dash for the bedroom and the satchel she had not yet unpacked, and pulled out the book. On the plane she had read about the castle's history for more than an hour, until it became too painful, knowing she would never be there again. Knowing that each hour was taking her farther away.

Frantically she leafed through and pulled out a sheet of notepaper he had left in the book with some dates and references. It was written in the handwriting that was so familiar to her—the handwriting from the letters. Turning to the inside cover of the book, the signature leaped out at her like a bullet to the heart. M. Thomas Reese. That same small, neat handwriting Katherine knew so well.

Katherine reeled and had to sit on the edge of her bed. Confusion and disillusion assailed all her senses, but gradually the truth started to seep through.

The truth. Mike had never written to her before this note that arrived today! He hadn't even remembered her complete address. All those other letters, all those years, had not been from Mike. She had been writing to his father!

If, indeed, it was Thomas who had been writing to her for four years, this explained so many things. The poetry Mike was so reluctant to read . . . the illness that had made no sense . . . the confusion over his marriage . . . the slip about his divorce. . . .

She let out a small cry. Anger rushed in like a hot wind. The nerve of him lying to her, pretending. Katherine crushed the letter, feeling the heat behind her eyes. He and his father had made such a fool of her!

Her mind whirled to dizziness. *Why would they do this? Why would they lie to her?* Anger gnawed and burned. They had been playing a game with her—a cruel and stupid game.

Katherine, insulted and infuriated, carried the book and the crumpled letter to her desk in the study. She stood staring at the photo of the man in the canoe, the photo she had gazed at so often, her man of letters. It was not a photograph of Mike. The photo was his father in his younger years.

"Thomas, I could kill you!" she said to the photograph. "I trusted you! Why would you do this?"

Why, if Thomas wrote those letters, had he never mentioned that his son was there with him in Wales? The omission was extremely odd, in retrospect.

He had deliberately misled her, no question about it. He had been charming and even romantic. *Why?* Katherine turned the photo facedown on the desktop. Could it be his age? He didn't want her to know? Ridiculous!

And puzzling. Mike had no reason on earth to pretend to be Thomas. The plot must have been his father's idea. Must have been, but how Mike had been cajoled into participating was hard to imagine. He had done it, though. Mike had lied and kept on lying. "Why would you lie to me, Michael?"

Thinking back, Katherine realized that when Mike first met her, he hadn't even read her letters. He couldn't have, because he made too many mistakes. The fact that Mike was so ill-informed was further evidence that he wasn't the originator of the scheme.

Later, though, he got better. Later, he made some references to things she had written. Katherine regretted ever having received the express letter from Manchester. It would have been better if she had never known. Better if she could have looked back on the memory of Mike and truly believed that in his own way, for a few short weeks one summer, he had really loved her.

She walked out into the sunshine, trying to deal with the pain. By now the worst of the anger had ebbed away. Only the heartbreak was left. The sweet memories had turned sour. Perhaps a time would come when she could look back on their moments of love and tenderness, and value those moments only for themselves, forgetting the game that was going on all the while, behind her back.

If Mike did telephone, as he promised, she would have to confront him and tell him what he and his father had done was unforgivable. When he said they should talk, no doubt he was referring to the lie. Funny he'd screw up on the handwriting. Or maybe he did that deliberately so she would figure it out and he wouldn't have to confess.

The smell of honeysuckle was strong in the summer air. Katherine breathed deeply of the fresh morning. The ache in her heart was a throbbing, physical pain. "God help me, I love him," she said aloud for the first time, making herself face it. "I love him and I always will."

This was going to be tough, but she would get through it. Right now she would force herself to face the world she had returned to and the day that loomed ahead. Whether her heart was here in Allendale or not, she had to get on with living. Today was just the beginning of life after Mike, and it was depressingly symbolic of a day in Rosalind's world—the world she had grown up in and had never been able to accept.

Like the required small dose of it this morning. She had a damn party dress to buy. Katherine tried not to think about Mike's promise to phone, but she was kidding herself. It was impossible not to long for the sound of his voice. And, under the circumstances, impossible to respect herself for wanting to hear him one more time.

That evening the phone did not ring. His message must not have been so urgent, after all. Two days passed. By the morning of Rosalind's party, Mike still had not called. So much for that promise. Just another in a series of lies.

STRAINS OF MUSIC floated out over the flower-decked garden. The orchestra, in white tuxedos with pink bow ties, played while guests mingled on the decks and lawns of the country club. Every family of status in the county was represented, the women in long gowns of summer organdies and voiles and linens and lace, and flower-trimmed hats. Tables were spread with a vari-

ety of caterer's delights. Under pink and green cano-
pies, ice sculptures melted slowly in the heat of the
August afternoon. Rosalind flitted about the garden
like a bird in pale yellow ruffles of dotted swiss.

Katherine was late. The alterations on the dress
Cecilia Stuart had sold her, with vocal misgivings, took
longer than estimated. White organdy patterned with
large leaves in three shades of green, the gown was set
around the neck with wide ruffles. Its full skirt was
tiered at the bottom. "It isn't exactly you," Cecilia had
told her with a strained expression on her face, and
Katherine had answered, "When I'm finished with it, it
will be."

Cecilia hadn't even wanted to show her this frock
because it was so unusual. But Katherine had liked the
fabric and the colors; she had seen the possibilities.

At home, Katherine had thrown herself into renovating a gown. Why not something frivolous and
pretty? The rest of her world had gone dark and cold.
And lonely.

She had removed all the ruffles from the bodice,
leaving a simple, plunging neckline. The skirt tier was
taken off. So what if she was the only woman in a short
dress? The frock had been transformed into bold glam-
our. It called for very high heels and a pearl brooch
worn at the waist. And a white flower for her hair.

A daring dress. Hardly the sort of thing the town
spinster would turn up in. While Katherine showered
that morning, it was the only garment hanging in her
guest-room closet. The heap of discarded clothes had
been transferred to cardboard boxes and piled in the
garage to give away. Symbols of her old life, discarded.

When she arrived a little late to the party, heads turned in her direction with small gasps of surprise. Rosalind tore away from a group of guests to sweep to her sister's side.

"Kath, what's happened to you? You're stunning! You found *that* dress in Allendale?"

"More or less," she answered.

Rosalind leaned in closer and whispered, "You are my sister Kathy, aren't you? Yipes, what that gown does for your figure! And your hair! Do you feel vibes of envy all around you? I love those envy vibes. Oh, this is great!" Her whisper got lower still. "I don't know what happened to you in Britain, but something did, and I'm bursting bursting bursting to hear it!"

"It's only a dress, Roz."

"You know better. Look at you!" Rosalind turned anxiously. "Oh, my goodness, Senator Martin and his wife have arrived! I must go. Mingle, Kath, mingle and flaunt. A waiter should be around any second with the champagne."

Katherine found that all the old friends and colleagues she ran into were aware that she had spent the past weeks in Britain. Roz had spread it all over town, and from what Katherine could surmise from their questions, her sister had implied that this was "yet another" of her European summers. Roz never quit. But Katherine understood how important it was to Roz, and the relief to finally be able to mention her sister's summertime whereabouts.

It was an agonizing chore for Katherine to mingle and flaunt and engage in impersonal party dialogues. Did these people mingling over champagne, putting on such airs, really impress each other? she wondered. Listening to less than half of what was being said, Katherine escaped the boredom by returning in her mind to the dark, cold fortress in the Welsh countryside that she had learned to love more than any other place on earth.

Nothing could have suited her bleak mood less than having to be here. Normally, Katherine wouldn't have allowed herself to suffer this way, but she owed the day to her sister, because her presence at the party was so important to Roz. Still, endless hours loomed before her. The biggest party of the season always lasted until long after the lights had been turned on in the gardens, after the long summer twilight. For the socialites of Allendale, when this celebration ended, so ended the leisure days of summer.

Half an hour later Katherine stood on an ornate stone bridge that arched over a pond full of lily pads. The lawn sloped sharply down from this spot, past flowers and splashing fountains, toward the stately, redbrick, white-pillared country club. She was talking with old school chums, now members of the country-club set. One, a lawyer, was discussing a real-estate investment he had made. The other, now wife of the town's pediatrician, was cutting in with questions about lake property. The orchestra was playing "Send in the Clowns."

Suddenly a strange rumble sounded around her—the rumble of whispers buzzing like electricity. The lawyer and the pediatrician's wife became mute and stood staring past Katherine, to the slope. Every person in the vicinity was looking toward the stone path behind her that circled around the lower garden and up toward the bridge on which she was standing.

Katherine turned. Her heart jumped as if it would leave her chest.

The object of the stares was a stunningly handsome young man who was walking up the path from the lower gardens, wearing skintight jeans and a half-buttoned white shirt with the sleeves rolled up past the elbows.

14

MIKE?

Mike was walking up that path! In his hand he carried a bunch of wildflowers picked from the hillsides of Wales—flowers she recognized—and his light eyes were sweeping over the crowd, looking for her.

The chatter around her had hushed. Every eye was on the handsome stranger. Women nudged each other and exchanged quick glances. Katherine, in shocked surprise, stood speechless.

He raised his head toward the bridge and saw her silhouetted against the sun, in white organdy, the flower in her hair, and halted as if he'd hit a wall. Then his arm raised in a wave.

She waved back. The silence around her turned to a rumble once again, but this time she did not hear anything but the thundering of her own heart. Too stunned to move, Katherine stood on the bridge and watched his walk quicken to a run. She was aware of hot sun on her shoulders and the sun's rays in her eyes, and she thought, *I'm hallucinating! He is a mirage caused by the sun's rays and my imagination. I have lost my grip on reality!*

But he didn't disappear when she blinked; he was drawing nearer by the second. Her heart beat wildly. She heard voices around her, knew eyes were fixed on her from all directions...so it must mean everyone else could see him, too.

And still she couldn't move. Mike sprinted onto the bridge. He pulled her into his arms without a word, and held her as if he never wanted to let go. The secure and perfect joy of being in Mike's arms—sensations Katherine believed had been lost forever—had not been lost, not yet. Her world spun in gold again.

Pandemonium broke out. Guests, all gaping and chattering at once, sounded like a colony of geese.

"Mike," she whispered into his chest as he held her. "Mike...what are you doing here?"

He answered, "I've come to take you home."

Katherine's heart jumped, stopped, and jumped again. *What was he saying?* "How...did you find me?"

"The cab driver knew about the party and told me you'd be here."

"I can't believe...you came...all this way...."

"I brought you some flowers from our hill." He held the bouquet out to her. The spicy scent of the wildflowers took her back to the windblown moors where they had run together. For a moment she could feel the cool wind in her face and hear the rushing stream and the soft bleating of the sheep.

She accepted the flowers, looking up at him. "You've carried these all the way across the ocean."

"I'd have carried them across the world for you." Mike circled his arms around her once again. Softly into her ear, he whispered, "I'm crazy in love with you. I can't live a day more without you."

Had he not been holding her, she might have fallen. A breath that was half sigh and half sob caught in her throat. The emotional overload was so overwhelming she was unable to respond until she could get a full breath again.

"Will you come home with me?" he said.

"Mike, I . . . you're confusing me. . . ."

His body tensed. "Is it too soon to ask? Or not soon enough? I should have said this before you left. I tried to catch you. I was afraid it wasn't right—wasn't what you really wanted. . . ."

She pulled gently away from his embrace. Suddenly aware of the stares around them, Katherine flushed. Mike had whispered; no one had heard anything either of them had said, but she knew all these people would try to interpret her every move. The unexpected reunion with the man she loved was hideously public and her emotions were barely in control. She wanted to run from the eyes, and couldn't. Didn't dare.

Instead, she whispered, "I'm not sure . . . who you are."

His gaze set on hers. "What does that mean? You know me better than anyone ever knew me."

"Through your letters, you mean?"

He stared. She stared back. The crowd behind and around them was whispering and tittering.

He closed his eyes, then opened them slowly. "You know?"

"Yes. What I don't know is why."

Shaken, Mike took her hand. "Where can we go to talk?"

Before Katherine could answer, Rosalind had swept down upon them like a bird of prey.

"What on earth," she was gasping, "is going on?"

Trying to calm her quivering voice, Katherine answered, "Roz, this is Michael Reese. Michael, my sister, Rosalind."

Rosalind could only stammer, "Who?"

Katherine knew exactly what it would take to distract her sister from her initial outrage over their long public embrace. She said, "Michael is lord of Castle Aawn."

Eyes glazing with disbelief, Rosalind caught her breath and nearly tumbled backward over the bridge. "Lord of the castle? You are Michael?"

"I am."

"Oh, my God."

He said, "I'm just off the plane and not dressed for a party, for which I apologize."

"Mike and I are leaving," Katherine said. "We have some things we want to discuss."

"Well, good heavens, can't you talk a little later? People want to meet Michael. They're absolutely dying of curiosity. Just look around. Have you ever seen such a reaction in your life? Oh, I love this. You must introduce him, Kath, love. When they find out Michael is the lord of—"

"Later, perhaps. Right now, you'll have to excuse us," Katherine insisted, clutching Mike's hand.

She led him down off the bridge and through a white wrought-iron gate into a fenced garden that was isolated from the main area by hedges and high trees. The lush private garden was sometimes used for small breakfast gatherings. They sat on a stone bench under the shade of a weeping willow. She held the bouquet of wildflowers on her lap.

"I want to take you in my arms and kiss you," Mike said. "But you'll push me away, won't you? You're angry, and I don't blame you. How did you find out?"

"The handwriting in your express letter. I had never seen it before."

"I was too stupid even to think of that. I was so mad at myself for letting you get away. I was going crazy. I'm crazy in love with you. I should have told you before."

"I would have believed you. Why didn't you tell me?"

"That I loved you? I thought you couldn't love a guy like me . . . who lives as I do . . . where I do."

Across the garden, the orchestra was playing "Unchained Melody." Katherine pulled herself into the strains of the music, trying to lose herself in it, as if it might offer some little buffer from the shock of his deceit.

Mike said, "I owe you an explanation about the letters. It was a ridiculous idea Dad manipulated me into. I'm not trying to weasel out of the blame. The blame is as much mine as his. But the idea was his."

"I figured as much. But you're a big boy. You didn't have to play."

"I felt like I did, at the time. Dad had misrepresented his age. He couldn't face your disappointment when you met him. Or his own embarrassment."

"But that's . . . that's crazy."

"Not to him. He used the sympathy ploy on me and it worked. He said it was the last favor he'd ever ask of me before he dies." Mike touched her hand. "We argued about it. I didn't want any part of it, believe me."

"Knowing you, I do. But you did it. I feel like an idiot. Do you know how humiliating this is?"

"It's humiliating for me, too. For everybody. I'm the one who should feel like a fool . . . and I do. You were the unsuspecting victim."

"And still confused. Thomas never mentioned his son was there. Who was at the castle first?"

"He was. He found the castle and we both financed it. Dad had no plans for the hotel, though. That was my idea, after I got to Aawn two years later. When I saw the castle, I knew it was where I wanted to be. That was when the renovation began."

"It all falls into place now."

He scowled. "You don't know how tough it was for me to let you think lies about me. I hated it. It's hard to believe I let myself get involved in something so childish."

Katherine saw his pain. Mike had never been good at hiding pain. She sighed shakily. "How ill is your father?"

"He's had two serious heart attacks and his blood pressure is far too high. His health is cause for worry."

"Protecting him was more important than telling me the truth . . . even later, after you and I became close?"

"Yes, but it wasn't a judgment call. I came within an inch of telling you about our dumb identity switch, because as soon as I realized you and I had feelings for each other, I couldn't take any more of it. I insisted on telling you. Dad pleaded with me not to. He said he couldn't face you, and it was true, he couldn't. I had to spare him having to face you. By then it was too late to gracefully get out of the hole we had dug." He winced. "I apologize, Kathy. It was a rotten trick."

She felt tears forming behind her eyes, and fought to keep them back. "Would you ever have told me?"

"Hell, of course I would have! As hypocritical as it might sound, I believe in honesty above all else."

She fell into silence. The sun shone through the willow branches, making light and dark shadows around them. The orchestra across the fence was playing a medley of songs from the seventies.

He continued, "And now I'm going to contradict my last statement by asking you not to tell Dad that you know. I hate like hell to see him hurt even though this whole mess was his idea in the first place."

She swallowed. "I can understand that, Mike."

He straightened. "Can you? Can you really?"

"Protecting your dad's dignity isn't difficult to understand. I wouldn't want to hurt him, either. I suppose if we had parted forever the day I left, it would have been better left as it was...my never knowing the difference. I still wouldn't know the truth if you hadn't sent the letter."

"All I was thinking about was you and me and how much I wanted you with me forever."

Their eyes met.

He said softly, "I always knew you would understand, not because I deserve understanding, but because of the person you are—the woman I've fallen in love with. A woman whose values are the same as mine and whose heart has touched mine. Can you love me, Kathy? Do you?"

"You know I love you or you wouldn't have come."

He exhaled a great, loud breath. "You'll come home? You'll marry me? Can you be happy at the castle with me?"

Her joy soared. His words were ringing like a tolling bell. Katherine clutched at the flowers and looked into his eyes. "I'd rather live at your castle with you than anywhere else in the universe."

"That's a yes! You said yes!" Mike pulled her into his arms and kissed her deeply.

He reached into his pocket and produced a small velvet box. "I had to choose this ring hurriedly, my sweet. But with more thought and care than you'll ever know."

Three large diamonds in a setting of gold flashed like fire in the sun. Carefully he placed the ring on her finger.

Katherine gazed in disbelief. "It's . . . beautiful," she whispered. "How can it be that only an hour ago I thought I would never see you again?"

She was afraid to take her eyes away, for fear when she looked back, the sparkling diamonds would be gone and she would wake from this dream that her knight of nights had come to take her home to his medieval castle.

"You'll have to give up your career," he said.

She smiled. "I can still study legends all I like, but I'd rather help you build and run your castle inn. What could be more wonderful?"

"Nothing could. When will you marry me?"

This question caught her completely off guard. "When?"

"I was thinking on the plane that if you did consent to marry me, we should do it here. Less red tape for Americans in America. And your family is here."

Katherine's breath left her. Her head was spinning. It was all happening too fast. "You're in a great hurry?"

"Patience isn't one of my virtues," he answered. "Please tell me you don't believe in long engagements."

"Not with me here and you over there."

"Then let's do it! When? Tomorrow?"

"Oh, I can't think right now!" Still holding the bouquet, Katherine threw her arms around him. "This is just beginning to sink in."

She jumped up, took his hand and pulled him to his feet. "Come on! We must find Roz and tell her!"

The music grew louder as they walked through the hedges and the gate, back into the heart of the party. Heads turned.

"I hope you can stand being stared at," she said.

"The way I'm dressed doesn't help."

"You're right, but not for the reason you think."

He grinned. She thought, *he knows exactly what he looks like in those jeans.*

Roz, smiling broadly, came across the lawn to meet them halfway between a bed of peonies and a sparkling fountain.

"At last you two have surfaced! Michael, everybody is dying to meet Katherine's mysterious friend! You must—"

"Katherine's fiancé," he corrected.

Roz's eyes widened. Her mouth flew open. She looked from the stranger back to her sister. "Is it true?"

Katherine held out her left hand. The diamonds sparkled with blinding radiance.

"I think I may faint! But you two just met this summer!" She grasped her sister's hand. "Didn't you?"

"It's been a very . . . magical summer," Katherine answered. Her happiness was only now merging with reality. "My ring is beautiful, isn't it?"

"Absolutely stunning! Oh, but this is wonderful! Look at the faces of these people, especially the women. Oh, Kath, you are the envy of them all! My Kath, the envy of every woman in Allendale! Wait until they hear the news! Oh, I love this. I love this. Every eye is on Michael and you. Kath, he's absolutely gorgeous. Michael, you're gorgeous. I'm going to make the announcement! Yes! An announcement. They'll ask when is the wedding? Have you set any date? We have a wedding to plan! You're marrying a prince!"

"Roz, hold it! I'm still coming down from the clouds myself. I don't want a big wedding. There isn't time."

Her sister's face paled. "What do you mean, there isn't time? You must have a big wedding!"

"We're going to be married right away. Mike has to get back home, and I'm going with him." *I'm ready to leave,* Katherine thought. *I don't belong here anymore. I've known it since I stepped off the plane. There is only one place I belong.*

"You can't just run off! It isn't fair. It would break my heart. Michael, do you have any idea how important a lovely wedding is to a woman?"

He frowned and turned. "Is it, Kathy?"

"I don't want to wait," she said. "It would take weeks to organize the kind of wedding Roz is talking about. I don't want to go through all that hustle and headache when I could be in Wales with you instead."

Roz lowered her voice to a whisper, to make sure she wasn't overheard. "What do you want, then? A pastel business suit with a corsage and a justice of the peace in his cigar-smelling back office?"

A cloud crossed Katherine's eyes. "Don't be morose."

Tears formed in Rosalind's eyes. Roz wanted her to have a lovely wedding, Katherine realized, because she loved her. She reached for Roz's hand.

"Kathy," Mike said. "I think we should talk about this. I don't want to cheat you out of a wedding just because I'm impatient for us to be together."

"You must have a wonderful day to look back on for the rest of your life," her sister argued. "So you and I can curl up together on cold nights when we're too old to do anything else, and look back on our wedding days. Oh, Kath! Michael, do something!"

"But there isn't time," Katherine insisted weakly. Roz was telling her that forfeiting memories was a decision one could never take back. It would be wonderful to have a day to remember. A lovely ceremony, perhaps in a beautiful garden...like this...with music and champagne and friends...like this...exactly like this.... If she were to plan the perfect wedding, it would be just like Roz's garden party, with all the flowers and the—

"All right, then!" Katherine agreed, with a burst of inspiration. "What could be more perfect than this setting? Or this day? We couldn't do better than this if we planned for a year! Would you be up to it, Roz? Mike, would you?"

Rosalind blinked. Her eyes were shining brightly. "Here? Now?"

Mike squeezed Katherine's hand. "It sounds terrific! All I'd need is the proper attire. Kathy's right—what could be better? What about it, Rosalind?"

Roz's mouth opened and closed like a puppet's. "Good heavens, I love it! A surprise wedding! People will be talking about this party for decades! It will rock the foundations of the town. You will be such a beautiful bride, Kathy! I've never seen you look as beautiful as you look today. Yes! Oh, absolutely yes! Can we really do it?"

"Maybe not," Mike said. "There's the matter of blood tests and license."

"To my knowledge," Katherine answered, "there's no law that requires the license before the ceremony. This came up two or three times at the circus, on the road. The ceremony is a private thing. It's the license that makes a marriage legal. We'll do the ceremony first and get the license afterward. What difference does it make?"

"None to me," Mike said. "As far as I'm concerned, you became my wife the moment you said yes."

Trembling with excitement, Rosalind pulled Mike's wrist toward her to look at his watch. "How much time do we need? Mike, you need a tux. No problem, our friend who runs a men's store is here. We'll need a few more flowers, also no problem. Paul Sands of Sands Flowers is here. Our minister is here. We even have a hired photographer already here. The country club does weddings all the time—they have plenty of chairs. The orchestra might want to confer on the music. With our connections I'm sure we can get a marvelous cake. And Kath, you'll wear Mother's wedding gown, like I did, like you always said you would. It's hung carefully in my closet waiting for you. Two hours will be ample time. The party is young yet. Oh, I love it! I must make the announcement at once!"

She hurried toward the stage, where she stopped the orchestra and stepped up to the microphone. "Everyone! Everyone! Your attention, please! It is my pleasure to announce the betrothal of my sister, Katherine, to lord Michael Reese of Great Britain. Katherine has just returned from a visit to Michael's castle in Wales, and he has joined her today for their wedding."

She waited for the rumble of startled voices to wane. It was a long wait. She held up her hand. "Now for the best! The surprise we have been saving! Our friends, you are all invited to the wedding ceremony, which will take place in two hours right here, in the main garden!"

An uproar surged from the crowd. This time their hostess had to raise both arms to try to quiet the stunned guests. "Isn't it exciting? Have more champagne, everyone! This promises to be a memorable day!"

Over the bluster of applause, Mike said to his fiancée, "Lord Michael?"

Katherine winced. "I should have known better than to kid about it. Roz doesn't miss the slightest opportunity."

"It's fraudulent and ridiculous."

Katherine laughed. "She's terribly proud of you. Roz knows the difference between a castle lord and a titled lord and doesn't care. She grasped onto the word because of the impression it would make."

He shrugged. "Hell, who cares? All I care about is that before this day is over, you're going to be my wife. If a hundred people weren't looking at us right now, I'd kiss you ravenously. I sure look the part of a lord, don't

I? Where is my fairy godperson—this owner of a men's shop?"

"Right over there. Roz has already flagged him down. Transform yourself, Michael of Aawn. And so will I. And I'll see you in two hours' time."

IMMACULATELY ATTIRED in a gray tuxedo, Mike awaited his bride beside a fountain that caught sparks of sun like diamonds. Before him, on the green velvet lawn, chairs seating more than a hundred guests had been placed on each side of an aisle. On Mike's right, standing behind a giant arrangement of roses, stood the smiling family minister, dressed in a white robe. The orchestra was playing a medley of love songs, until, on signal, the music paused. And the wedding march began.

Rosalind, dressed in a flowing pink gown—the same gown Katherine had worn in her wedding—walked slowly down the long aisle.

Mike caught his breath at the sight of his bride. Katherine, on the arm of her brother-in-law, shimmered in shell-white satin and lace. She carried the bouquet of wildflowers from the hills above Aawn.

For Katherine, the scene before her was a blur. The smiling faces of the guests, many of whom were her lifelong friends. The wide satin ribbons strung along the aisle chairs. Roz in front of her, walking slowly, turning with smiles for everyone. The minister who had baptized her. The sparkling sprays of the fountain.

Only Mike was clearly in focus. His eyes were fixed on her as she walked slowly toward him.

The day had spun so out of orbit it was scarcely real. Almost impossible to experience for itself. The bride found herself thinking not of the old life, from which this moment she was walking away, but of the life she was walking into. The life each step was bringing her closer to.

Mike was a picture before her—a beautiful picture, not quite real. Even now as she was walking down the aisle, Katherine was thinking of him against a backdrop of gray stone curtains. She was thinking of the subtle smell of his cologne in winding tower stairwells, when he took her hand in the dark. She thought of the two of them running with the dogs on the wild moors.... With every step, Katherine was leaving her old world behind.

Mike moved forward before she had reached the bank of roses that marked the end of the aisle. When Rusty stepped back, Mike, shrugging off protocol, reached toward his bride and took her hand, and didn't let go, not even when, to her surprise, he produced a gold wedding band.

"I'll always keep you warm," Mike said as he placed the band on her finger.

She smiled, realizing that he, too, in his thoughts, was already home. With her.

THEY STOOD on the battlements of the gatehouse tower, gazing out over the waters of Tywyllyn and green hills beyond.

"How lucky I am," Katherine said.

"How lucky we both are. This castle plunged into a state of mourning when you went away."

"I won't ever leave again." Katherine leaned against the warm, solid body of her husband. "Well, only for a few days to clear up my affairs after Rusty gets my house sold."

Mike said, "I still marvel that you love me. That you love my castle as much as I do."

Her eyes were dreamy. "Mike, how did you know the dragon wouldn't frighten me away?"

"Because I know him . . . and I know you. You approve of each other. It's as simple as that."

"Would he approve of children tearing around and interfering with the peace of his lair?" she asked. The surprise showed on Mike's face as he turned toward her.

Katherine continued, "You've never brought up the subject. Do you ever think about having a child?"

He stared at her. "Do you?"

"Yes."

He grinned. "That's great! That's great, Kathy. Then we'll do it!"

A moon was shining white and pale in the silver of a long August twilight. Behind them the topmost tower walls embraced the shadows. The archway to the enclosed stairway opened to a circular hall of darkness where steps spiraled down and down into the castle depths.

"It's so eerie the way the wind catches and moans in the tower," she said.

"There is no wind," he answered.

"No wind? Then what is that sound?"

They listened to a windlike flapping, soft and then softer still, and then louder again.

"What is it?" she whispered. "Is it him?"

"Yes," Mike said softly. "It's his wings moving."

Tiny echoes like clicks, each click more echo than sound, whispered in pitch-dark passages of stone, soft against the gentle sigh of wings.

Katherine held her breath and listened. The strange, moaning breeze that blew through the stairwell felt warm against their faces.

"Let's go down and see if we can see him," Mike said, taking his wife's hand in his. "Our dragon has come out to welcome us home."

This August, don't miss an exclusive
two-in-one collection of earlier love stories

MAN
WITH A PAST

TRUE COLORS

by one of today's hottest
romance authors,

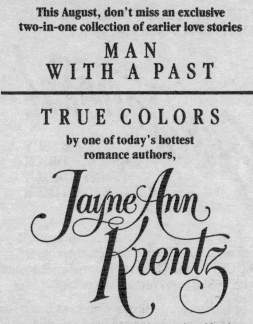

Jayne Ann Krentz

Now, two of Jayne Ann Krentz's most loved books are
available together in this special edition that new and
longtime fans will want to add to their bookshelves.

Let Jayne Ann Krentz capture your hearts with the love
stories, MAN WITH A PAST and TRUE COLORS.

And in October, watch for the second two-in-one
collection by Barbara Delinsky!

Available wherever Harlequin books are sold.

HARLEQUIN
Romance®

Back by Popular Demand

Janet Dailey
Americana

A romantic tour of America through fifty favorite Harlequin Presents, each set in a different state researched by Janet and her husband, Bill. A journey of a lifetime in one cherished collection.

In August, don't miss the exciting states featured in:

Title #13 — ILLINOIS
        The Lyon's Share

#14 — INDIANA
        The Indy Man

Available wherever
Harlequin books are sold.

Take 4 bestselling love stories FREE

Plus get a FREE surprise gift!

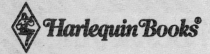
Harlequin Books®

GREAT NEWS...
HARLEQUIN UNVEILS NEW SHIPPING PLANS

For the convenience of customers, Harlequin has announced that Harlequin romances will now be available in stores at these convenient times each month*:

Harlequin Presents, American Romance, Historical, Intrigue:

> May titles: April 10
> June titles: May 8
> July titles: June 5
> August titles: July 10

Harlequin Romance, Superromance, Temptation, Regency Romance:

> May titles: April 24
> June titles: May 22
> July titles: June 19
> August titles: July 24

We hope this new schedule is convenient for you.

With only two trips each month to your local bookseller, you'll never miss any of your favorite authors!

*Please note: There may be slight variations in on-sale dates in your area due to differences in shipping and handling.

*Applicable to U.S. only.

HDATES-RR